When No One Came

Skyy Banks

Columbus, Georgia, USA

www.urbanedgepublishing.com

Copyright © 2015 by Skyy Banks
Cover Design: Keith Saunders
Edited by: Giovanni Dortch, Zenzilé's Way Consulting

All rights reserved. This book or any portion thereof may not be reproduced or used in any manner whatsoever without the express written permission of the publisher except for the use of brief quotations in a book review.

Printed in the United States of America

First Printing, 2015

ISBN 978-0-9815326-0-8

Urban Edge Publishing
P.O. Box 6025
Columbus, GA 31917
www.urbanedgepublishing.com

DEDICATION

For all the missing brown boys and girls. You are not forgotten.

CONTENTS

DEDICATION iii

CONTENTS v

ACKNOWLEDGMENTS i

BITTERSWEET GOODBYE 1

STAKEOUT 6

MISSING PERSON #1 12

MISSING PERSON #2 23

INTRODUCING THE HAWKS 31

ADVANCED TRAINING 41

LOCKED AND LOADED 49

STAKEOUT #2 59

MISSING PERSON #1 72

UNWELCOME VISITOR 90

MISSING PERSON #2 96

MISSING PERSON #3 104

SHAKY GROUND 116

JANE DOE	124
HOLD THEM OR FOLD THEM	135
UNNECESSARY ROUGHNESS	142
GETTING AN UNDERSTANDING	161
JUSTICE NOT DENIED	168
TOO CLOSE FOR COMFORT	183
THE TAKEDOWN	204
WHO WILL CRY FOR THE CHILDREN?	219
ABOUT THE AUTHOR	

ACKNOWLEDGMENTS

With God all things are possible. As I wrote this book and thought about the countless number of children who become missing and exploited everyday I kept this text of scripture in the forefront of mind praying for their safe returns.

Thank you to all who labored with me as I birthed this book. There are not enough words to express my gratitude.

BITTERSWEET GOODBYE

Looking out over the endless acres of land, the breathtaking beauty of the fall foliage did not move Marissa from the state of utter despair that she had been engulfed by for the past two weeks. She had known hurt before. She knew exactly what it felt like, or so she thought. This pain was unbearable and unreachable.

"It's always beautiful this time of year." "It's always beautiful this time of year." Stepping closer, this time almost standing on Marissa's heels, Tressa's comment still fell on deaf ears. Her eyes were hollow-- sunk into her face. The phrase 'the eyes are the window to the soul' gained new meaning. Marissa's eyes were empty, and at this point, so was her soul, or so she felt. Death had knocked on their door before, but this time it was different. It was unexpected. They had no time to say their goodbyes. Right any wrongs if there were any.

Standing shoulder to shoulder, the pain they felt wouldn't allow for words. Questions of how and why swirled in their heads. Glazed eyes stared at a future that was uncertain. The muffled voices behind the study's French doors grew louder as more people arrived at the house. College friends, clients, family, sorority sisters and all who loved Olivia came to pay their respect.

"It's too dangerous this time." While the team had been in similar search and rescue operations, this one didn't feel right. Swaying slightly from side to side, Marissa replayed the sequence of events in her head trying to figure out how things went bad so quickly. How they had run the same play over a dozen times being sure to account for the unexpected and how they always returned safely, either plus one or taking down an entire set over the past three years. This would be the final run. They had decided it was time. Time to get back to their lives, to a sense of normalcy where they weren't constantly looking over their shoulders.

Marissa pleaded again, "I think we should turn around. It's obvious we are dealing with some people who are smarter and faster than we are. There has to be some big money behind this operation. Nothing is laid out as before. Just look around. Five men on patrol instead of two, where did the dogs come from?"

"Let's take what we have and just turn it over to the feds." Olivia offered a viable alternative that was sure to ease any apprehension, while, in their minds, ensuring that the mission would be accomplished.

"It's too much red tape. We need them to move quickly. If not, this house will be abandoned or burned to the ground when and if they do make it." Tressa refused to back down. "And you all know damn well that's not going to happen without us being interrogated and them- the men in black starting their own investigation on us. Hell, for all we know, to them we are a bunch of overzealous wanna be vigilantes. This war on children is not ours to fight alone."

"Vigilantes?" Gay smirked.

"You know what I mean. Come on now, let's get serious." Tressa sighed obviously frustrated. She was ready to make a move. Get in and get out.

"You sure you don't have balls? Because they get bigger every year." Gay continued with the snide remarks.

"It's called heart. I got it from you Mama bear. Are we done talking?"

Marissa rolled her eyes having previously tangled with Tressa about not knowing when enough was just that... enough. "We are across the border for God's sake... deep into cartel country and who knows what other illegal happenings."

Olivia continued to side with Marissa. "Right! We did just purchase some weapons. Lord knows I don't want to go to jail in Mexico. We're not trying to do some 'Set it Off' kinda shit. We have all the evidence. We know it's s about four or five kids in there all under eighteen."

"There have to be more." Gay spoke as though she was deep in thought contemplating the next move while listening to the conversation around her.

"If there are more, this very attempt to get them out could go one of two ways. We get them safely out or we don't, then they, along with God knows how many more kids would be trapped." Tressa painted the picture to be as dire as it was.

"Right, but who knows if the men in black aren't already on this?" asked Olivia.

"Believe me, if they were we would know about it."

With tears rolling down her cheeks and mucous draining from her nose, a motionless Marissa had reached that moment in her mind. The moment that time seemingly stood still.

Tiny legs dangled at her waist while tiny arms offered a grip that only fear could know. With the smallest girl on her back and two girls on either side Tressa ran as fast as she could across the yard of the makeshift compound to the awaiting van. The girl's hand was so tiny it slipped from Tressa's. "Keep going. I got her!" *Olivia yelled running a few feet behind with her own precious cargo.*

Scooping the girl in her arms, Olivia was a close second. The door of the van flew open. Held high by the owner, the double barrel shot gun on the other side of the door was locked, loaded, and ready to kill in an instant. The driver revved up the engine. Olivia hoisted the last girl into the van looked at Tressa who was comforting the little ones and smiled. Everything was happening so fast.

A black heel flew in the air. A loud thud followed a loud cry. Marissa's limp body lay underneath the windowsill. While she was not unconscious, she laid on her side motionless with her eyes closed breathing slow and steady. Kneeling down beside her, Tressa's hand made small comforting circles in the middle of her back. This time the big sister could do nothing to soothe the little sister.

"It's going to be okay baby." Tressa lied. Pained by guilt, she fought to hold the tears back. If she bit her lips any harder she would have definitely drawn blood.

"You've said that before." Opening her eyes, Marissa rolled over to her back as far as he could before being obstructed by Tressa's knees. "That's your favorite line. It's going to be okay, baby. This time it's more than falling off my bike and scraping my elbows or not making the cheerleading squad or getting my heart broken. Those were easy fixes."

"Yes."

"So tell me how it's going to be okay?"

"I can't and I'm so sorry." Marissa was right and Tressa knew it. There was no bandage big enough, no revenge scheme grand enough, no time machine to undo what had happened. "Baby girl, baby girl…" The salty tears seeped through her slightly parted lips.

"It's almost time." Gay's head appeared through the door. Seeing the women on the floor, she came inside. There were really no words to be spoken this time. Extending her hand to both of them she helped them to their feet. "It's almost time." Followed by a long group hug and more tears.

STAKEOUT

"Y'all are too funny." Gay laughed from the back seat. Her ombre locs swayed from side to side with her head movements as she talked. "Just remember who is doing what. We have to be on the same page with this. Rule number one of surveillance. Always let the right hand know what the left hand is doing."

"Is that a rule you wrote or did you really learn that somewhere? Inquiring minds, that would be all of us, want to know." Marissa teased.

This was the second night in a row that Gay had called the ladies to come hang out with her. 'Hanging out' usually meant work with her. GT Investigations had been going strong for six years now, but Gay hadn't found a partner that was good enough. The ladies always told her she probably never would because her standards were too rigid, especially with not wanting a male partner. Gay was a bit of a rebel, and was always out to prove a point.

"If you heifers must know, I coined that one myself. But it's true, kinda like a relationship. You have to be on the same page to always have each other's back."

"And you would know Miss Chronically Single." Tressa quipped.

"The classic pot calling the kettle black I see. Tsk-tsk." Gay couldn't help but laugh.

Olivia moaned. "See we go through this every time. Come on now let's get serious before we miss something. I'm ready to go home. You better be glad tomorrow is Saturday. I was about to 'no call- no show' on your behind."

The man Gay had under surveillance was a night owl and moved quite a bit. She needed someone who could be her eyes and ears while she rested.

Pulling at Gay's hair in a playful manner, "You're going to cause me to get a divorce if you keep this up or we are going to have to start inviting Jonathan to these midnight shindigs." Marissa jested.

Returning the favor, Gay pulled at the nape of Marissa's afro. "I'm open. You know I'm always looking for a good time, especially being chronically single. I've almost forgotten what a man looks like."

"See, I gotta watch you. You should've acted right when you had him. Your loss, my gain."

"I just had a flashback from UCLA."

"Don't start bringing up that old mess. I've grown since then. A little anyway." Gay giggled. "It was fun while it lasted. I knew he had a thing for you after about the second time he came over to the dorm."

"Really?" Marissa perked up.

"Yeah really."

The two had been friends since college. Gay hailed from Brooklyn and Marissa from Seattle. And from the very beginning the east and west coasts truly collided. From disagreements over space, to visitors in their dorm room, to guys, the two were constantly at each other's throat. Due to overcrowding they were stuck with each other for at least a semester.

"Yo, Ma. Thanks for letting him get away." Marissa showcased her best Brooklyn imitation.

"Thanks for taking us down memory lane ladies, but let's focus. My bed is calling me and 5:30 comes soon. I'm booked solid tomorrow with my first client at 7. You know these women don't play about their hair." Olivia tried to sound lively through her sleepiness.

"So why did you have to come out with your hair all tied up looking like an old lady?"

"Marissa you know I'm serious about this mane. It didn't get to be down my back by chance. I'm one of those women who don't play about her hair, humph."

Tressa sounded off. "Children, Can we get serious? All this memory lane - beauty shop talk has to end. We can do that at lunch or something. I have a few emergency patients to see in the morning and I'm not trying to do a root canal with one eye open."

"Okay- okay. Damn I forgot how smart you two sisters are, an engineer and a dentist. Go head Marissa and Tressa!"

Tressa laughed. "Gay you play too darn much. Now what are we supposed to be doing here exactly? I need to know what the left hand is doing."

"Well exactly. Hmmmm. Here's a quick rundown. There is a well-known real estate developer who's having an affair with a prominent public official. I will let you see for yourselves in a minute. The wife has hired me... us to get all the dirt because she's about to cash his ass in. That's it in a nutshell."

"And you get pleasure out of this?" Olivia asked, perplexed.

"Not that I get pleasure. I have a very unique set of skills that allows me to be compensated well. And I live in a city that is near other big cities that have all kinda wrong shit happening to good people or wrong shit happening to people that deserve it. Why not do what I know how to do best and get paid for it? You all do it. It just doesn't involve pulling people's cards. Showing who they really are."

"But you have to admit that digging for dirt on unfaithful spouses has to be the worst."

"Olivia my dear. It's only the worst when it's your spouse."

***

For almost two hours a single car did not enter or leave the boutique hotel they were watching. The full moon gave off a beautiful bluish glow illuminating the streets. The four of them sat in the car and took turns watching. The windows were cracked slightly to keep the humidity levels down and prevent the windows from fogging up. The winter air was cold and the whirring sound of the battery operated heaters coupled with being bundled in layers made it difficult to stay awake. All these measures were necessary to avoid attention to a running car on the side of the street in the middle of the night. Four women sitting in a car in the middle of the night was suspicious enough.

"We are going to give it one more hour and then call it a night."

"Thank you Warden Gay." Tressa offered sarcastically.

"You just have the camera ready missy, and Olivia, have the recorder ready to dictate what we see in detail."

"Aye, Aye, Captain." Olivia complied.

"I love these names- chronically single, warden, captain. You all are on a roll tonight. I owe you."

Just as they were reminded of their tasks, a tall man walked out of the front door of the hotel. Bundled in a trench coat, a scarf that covered much of his face and a fedora covering his head he walked briskly to the other side of the street with his hands shoved deep into the coat's pockets. Pressing the auto start, he looked around to ensure no one was watching before getting into the silver S- Class 4 door Mercedes.

Snapping away, Tressa captured his every move including the car tag that read *Mr. CEO*.

"Oh hell no!" Marissa hollered. "That is not who I think it is? There is only one man around town that drives a silver Mercedes with Mr. CEO tags."

"Ladies, see Mr. Parker Monroe of Parker Development Incorporated." Gay extended her hand in the direction of the parked car."

"You have to be freaking kidding me. How long have you been on this case?" Marissa was all ears. His firm had just landed a multi-million dollar deal with her company. They were set to build a new industrial complex outfitted with labs and onsite housing for visiting fellows and students. She had dined with him and his wife on several occasions, having been the lead project manager.

"It hasn't been long. But he's so sloppy. It won't take much longer. He leaves all kinds of paper trails and lets too many people handle his business. I think with the right amount of money, a whole lot of people could be singing." Gay entertained them.

Everyone was wide-awake at this point. Mr. Monroe sat in his car a while longer and appeared to be talking on the phone.

"Okay- here comes someone else." Olivia continued to take pictures.

A tall thin-framed woman walked out to the car that the valet had pulled around. The black 4-door Jaguar sedan fit her perfectly. There were no conspicuous car tags, just a simple and clean luxury car. She wore a dark purple trench coat with tall black boots. A close fit knit hat covered her head and a scarf covered much of her face. Driving off, Mr. CEO followed.

With a smirk, Gay's only response to what they witnessed was, "Let's go ladies. I don't think she's coming back tonight."

Marissa was still shocked at the discovery. "This is going to be wild when the shit finally hits the fan. I can't believe it! How long has he been cheating? Really?"

"Patience grasshopper. In due time, all will be revealed. We just have to move cautiously and silently. Now to get you professionals home."

MISSING PERSON #1

Hitting the floor with a padded thud, the condensation from the milk carton refused a steady hand. The opaque liquid snaked across the black and white mosaic tile. Jackie stood in the middle of the kitchen floor looking down at the emptying carton. For a brief moment, distracted by a movie playing on television, she had taken her eyes off the pot of cream of wheat simmering on the stove. The show on the Lifetime Movie Channel centered on a mother searching for her missing child. This was in the mid 80's. The milk carton in that scene bore the face of a Caucasian child with the words "Missing" and "Have You Seen Me" above the picture with a physical description that included height and weight below it with a key fact about the missing child beneath the description. Not until that moment had it dawned on her that efforts to find her baby girl had been futile. While she couldn't recall but a handful of incidences in her lifetime that gained widespread media attention, those incidences flashed in her mind as if they had occurred only yesterday- Polly Klaas and Jon Benet Ramsey. These were children from a world different than hers; children that mattered, so she believed. Every major television station had some kind of coverage before and after the children were found.

"Monroe County Sheriff's department."

"Detective Graham please," Stepping over the milk carton and its spilled contents she made her way to the cordless phone.

"He's not in the office. Would you like to leave a message?" The receptionist offered while recognizing an all too familiar voice.

"I've been calling every week like clockwork. It's always he's not in the office or there are no updates or they are following up on all leads. But nothing is happening. My child is still missing."

"Mrs. Mabrey, I assure you, we are working the case. There is only so much that we can do with the lack of staff and resources."

"Resources?"

"Yes, aside from listing Josalyn in the Missing Children's Clearinghouse, local and national databases, and partnering with schools, we also need physical bodies that can go out and talk to people, we need officers manning the phones all while maintaining their own caseloads."

"Would it be any different if she was white? If Josalyn was white?"

"Color has nothing to do with it. I assure you. It's just tough for everyone right now."

"Yes, you have made that point clear. And I beg to differ when not only two years ago Jon Benet Ramsey and her murder was all over the news. All kind of money was being thrown at the police and the community to find out who did it. Remember

Polly Klaas? Of course you do. How could anyone forget with her face plastered all over the news?" At that moment, all composure was gone. Misdirected anger escaped her as she felt her family was being given the short end of the stick after having seen the extremes undertaken by the police, the community and families of other missing children. The phone fell to the floor. Wailing she called out, "Josalyn!" This was the first time she had uttered her daughter's name in a long time to herself or anyone else. "Josalyn!"

Almost slipping on the spilled milk, Tony braced himself on the counter top to avoid falling as he rushed into the kitchen to see what the commotion was all about. Looking confused by the milk on the floor and the phone at Jackie's feet he asked, "Jackie, what's wrong baby?"

Shaking her head from side to side Jackie bent over with her hands resting on her knees. Tears communicated the ongoing hurt and despair she felt. Silence permeated the room except for the television and now the buzzing from the phone.

"Sit down baby." Guiding her to the table Tony pulled her chair out while pulling an adjacent one for him to sit beside her. Holding her hand, he asked again. "What's wrong? I didn't hear the phone ring. Is there bad news?" He could only assume the worse by Jackie's posture and the disarray of the kitchen.

"You know what's wrong. The question should be what's right? I called the station again and the same old mess but this time the mess comes along with excuses of why they can't or haven't done X, Y, Z. Save it!"

Beep, Beep. The sound from the smoke alarm interrupted the conversation. Tony turned to see smoke rising from the stove. "Hold on baby." Racing to the stove his heel caught the milk and he fell to the floor. "Damn." Jackie didn't move.

Her voice just above a whisper, "Josalyn. My baby has been gone for over a year now and nobody cares. All the posters have faded, the phone calls are few and far between, the award money is stuck at a measly $8,635.00, and that detective... You know if she wasn't black more would be done."

"Jackie we are not going to do this right now. Call me naïve but we can't say that it's because she is black. You want to compare our story to the ones in the news. We don't know everything about the families, their support network, their connections."

Jackie's anger spurred. "You don't live under a rock. If you are naïve it's because you choose to be. We don't have to know everything. The most important thing we don't know is where our daughter is, if she's dead or alive, and that very little if anything is being done about it."

"Point taken."

"And support system. Where are they? Phone calls asking questions won't do it. Hell how do they think I'm doing?"

"I don't want to fight. We're on the same team baby. Get dressed. I will clean this up." Having stayed up and cried many nights with his wife Tony refused to exacerbate the situation with empty words of comfort. The grief they were feeling could only be likened to a mother grieving the death of a child; the unknown fate made the anguish that much greater.

***

This was a regular meeting place- community parties, baby showers, bridal showers, birthday parties- just a place to celebrate each other and fellowship. Today was quite different. The large oak doors weren't welcoming; the cascading art on the walls didn't give off any warm fuzzies. This was the second time a meeting occurred that didn't involve laughter, balloons, good people and fun times outside of the regular neighborhood watch or home owner's association meeting. The room was full of black residents with a sprinkle of white ones throughout.

"Thank you for coming." Mr. Dinkins, the co- chair of the Home Owner's Association, called the meeting to order. "We wanted to give everyone an update on Josalyn Mabrey, the little girl that went missing at the end of summer, and to give reminder tips on how we can continue to keep the rest of our children safe. But before we do that I want to ask the Mabreys to come up and speak.

Nodding her head towards Tony, Jackie signaled him to go up and speak on their behalf. She was too drained, weary, mad, and a range of other emotions.

"Thank you all for coming. Thank you all for everything you have done. These past six or so months have been especially hard for us and to be honest sometimes we feel like we are in this all by ourselves. When Josalyn was first reported missing, we saw many of you almost everyday, some a few times a day from bringing food, to dropping off money, to find out how you could help. Now we may get a wave when we pass by or call here or there. What happened? She's still not home." Silence suffocated the room. Some people lowered their heads with guilt. He spoke a hurtful truth. "Many of you make think you don't have a dog in this fight but you do."

The doorbell chimed. Everyone looked around to see Detective Graham walk in. He had been a familiar fixture early on and could be seen patrolling the neighborhood during the times most children were out and about in the neighborhood- before school, after school and weekends.

"Excuse me, I apologize for being late but I just received notice of the meeting."

Mr. Dinkins greeted him. "No problem. We are glad you found time in your busy schedule. Come up if you don't mind and let us know what's going on."

"Sure." Walking past the crowd he nodded and shook hands on his way to the front of the room.

Tony continued, "As I was saying. Since we are a community we all have a vested interested in my daughter's disappearance. It could very well be one of you all one day. Think about it, we don't have a clue who could've taken her. For all we know it could be somebody right under all our noses."

"You right brother." Someone in attendance agreed.

"We talk about the village but where is the village. The concept still applies." His voice teetered towards anger and frustration reflecting on what Jackie had said earlier. "You aren't even talking to your children about it. Yes, I see more of you in the afternoons out with them or sitting in view but when your son or daughter stops by our home everyday and asks when is Josalyn coming home, that let's us know the conversation hasn't gone far enough."

Having made his way to the front of the room, Detective Graham stood by Mr. Mabrey while he continued to speak to the crowd and solicit their support beyond what had been given and offered an intermittent pat on the back for comfort and reassurance.

"I do appreciate you all for coming, although I expected more. Look around. Our subdivision alone has about 150 people who live there; this doesn't include the entire Rockport Community. Maybe it's true- not my child, not my problem. We tend to mind our own business until it's one of ours. That's oftentimes a little too late." With a lowered head he stepped aside, not before glancing up at Mrs. Mabrey's tear stained face.

"I too, thank you all for coming and as Tony said. "We have to do more. We have to stay vigilant, and we have to keep talking about it."

Mrs. Mabrey stood no longer able to keep quiet. "Detective Graham, I've called the office weekly staying on top of this case. Please tell me...tell us why you or the Monroe County Sheriff and Police Departments haven't done more, stayed vigilant and as you put it, continued to talk about it?"

Detective Graham's faced turned red. Pushing the cap on his head back to wipe the sweat from his brow, he stumbled over his words. "Yeeeesss, yeesss Mrs. Mabrey. I have received your messages and I do appreciate you calling and staying on top of us. I can't really give you a reason that would satisfy you as to why we have not been on top of it. A fact at this point would sound like an excuse. But the fact is we are understaffed, we don't have all the resources and equipment that the big cities have. That's we rely on you all to help us share the work."

Folding her arms across her chest, the petite 5 feet 3 inch tall woman stood straight and rebutted. "You may not have the resources but you do have connections and a phone. Law enforcement is a brother hood. It cost you nothing to pick up the phone and ask for some help this way. I know someone would come without a doubt."

Detective Graham was stuck. There was truth in what she said. He had not reached out and asked for help but instead put Josalyn's picture and description out on the wire as an all points bulletin- be on the lookout for... in addition to ensuring all neighboring county departments were faxed the same information to post in their stations.

Mrs. Mabrey gained support from the crowd that was beginning to grow restless. "Why haven't we gotten any updates about this case? You know the children who are old enough to understand are afraid and those too young to understand want to know why we are keeping them inside all the time." A parent asked anxiously.

"We have worked all the leads we have for now. We are still working the phones and covering all bases. It's not easy to call and report that there is nothing new in the case. But if it makes everyone feel better, we will. And you are right Mrs. Mabrey; we will reach back out to the neighboring offices and see if they can get a few people to assist."

"Did you question everyone in the subdivision? I don't recall you stopping by our house?" Another anxious parent asked.

"Again you are right. We haven't visited all the homes. But we do encourage anyone who might have seen something out of place, heard something, or saw an unfamiliar face or car to stop by or call the hotline. You may think of it as a small thing, but it could be something that could break this case wide open."

The creaking of chairs under shifting and moving weight could be heard along with pockets of conversation. The folks who had gathered expressed their concern amongst one another while tuning Detective Graham out. The more he spoke the less confident the people became in his abilities to handle the case.

"I understand your concern."

"Understanding isn't enough. We really need answers and actions." The president of the homeowner's association stood.

Dressed in a dark A-line dress that hung just above her knees; she was well polished with not a strand of hair out of place. The orange colored lipstick was a nice contrast to her tan skin and dark brown hair. She had promised to keep a candle burning for Josalyn until she came home and was one of the few that printed and replaced the posters when the rain had damaged them. What's next?" Mrs. Rainer pressed.

"What's next?" Detective Graham repeated as he searched for the right response that would satisfy the residents as well as give him more credibility and rebuild trust with a community that largely didn't look like him. "Mobilization and awareness. I think it's time we take this back to the press. We also need to do some canvassing of the area and nearby towns. With all the community happenings, people from nearby towns do come over."

By this time all attention was directed towards the front. He was now speaking a language they wanted to hear- action. "What do you mean by canvassing?" A lone man with a child asked.

"Canvassing is going door to door, business to business to inform people about Josalyn's disappearance and to ask questions. Have they seen her, have they seen any strange people and cars in the area recently or during that time? Ask them to donate to the reward fund. All these things are critical and doable but it has to be organized."

"What are the funds used for?" Someone from the back stood and asked.

"We use the money to provide cash rewards to those who provide important information leading to the arrest of the perpetrator, leading us to Josalyn or anything that will significantly impact the case. We can also use money for printing posters, setting up command posts, providing snacks and beverages to volunteers and things of that nature. Most of the time the latter is donated, keeping the money in the pot to attract those who may just know something but are waiting on the pot to grow. Unfortunately there are people like that out there.

"I'm ready."

"Me too."

"How do we get started?" Solidarity grew as the residents voiced their support.

Standing again to address those in attendance Mrs. Mabrey's demeanor had changed. A simple calm had replaced the onslaught of emotions she previously felt. "Thank you all. I just want to paint a picture of Josalyn for you, especially those who didn't know her. In hopes that after today you will remember her. That it won't be until the next meeting that you make a donation, post a sign or knock on a door. That it won't be until the next meeting that you remember Josalyn Nicole Mabrey, our only daughter."

For a second time the entire room was completely silent besides the occasional sound of a chair moving.

"Josalyn is a sweet rambunctious little girl who loves cream of wheat, butterflies, and turning cartwheels. She loves back rides from her dad even though she's getting older. She loves to sit at my feet while I read and read along. Her favorite subject is science and she's going to be a scientist. We are finally going to get her that puppy for her 11th birth…"

Reality hit Jackie like a ton of bricks. Josalyn's 11th birthday was in a few months. That reality paralyzed her to the point at which she couldn't speak. Leaning forward, the chair she used to support her weight gave way and she tumbled over. Gasps could be heard around the room. Tony ran down to his wife who was already being attended to.

"Let's get her some air. Can someone bring a wet napkin? Some water?" Tony asked for help while lifting her to a chair. "Please can we get some air?"

The residents stepped back but continued to watch what was going on. Some were crying others were on the phone and a few talked with Detective Graham and Mrs. Rainer. The energy was high in the room. Josalyn's disappearance had finally taken a toll on Jackie.

MISSING PERSON #2

Daylight savings time meant that the streetlights would come on a little later and the neighborhood kids had a little more time to hang out. This meant socializing and doing nothing more than catching up on what happened during the school day or the night before. A few bikes whizzed around the cul-de-sac as the younger kids weaved in and around the older ones trying to get the last basketball game in under the falling sun.

Standing on the curb, Dynasty's voice boomed over the other girls. "I have my outfit for the dance. I just may be the flyest chic in the place." Pulling at her freshly done twist out hair style and resting most of her weight on one leg in a way that pushed her hip to one side she boasted. Known for her athleticism, good looks and brains, being the leader of the pack wasn't a hard feat. Envied by her peers seemed to be an understatement.

"Dynasty Langston I'm not going to let you outdo me this time," joked Macy. "It's high time you share the shine. I don't know why you are being all secretive about your outfit either. Probably trying to show all those legs off."

"Macy Smith, don't start. I'm going to hook you up. We

all gotta represent." Macy and Dynasty had been friends since Kindergarten and were inseparable. Known as the odd couple around school one could hardly be seen without the other.

"Come over and help me convince momma to let you do my face."

"Now you know that answer gonna be no. But I'll try."

"When?"

"Gymnastics practice is tomorrow so I'll come Wednesday. Get her to fix lasagna."

"Watch out." Running to stop the loose ball before it hit the girls Aaron called out.

"You did that on purpose. Just trying to get by Dynasty."

With a smile that stretched from ear to ear and the retrieved ball pressed to his stomach, Aaron stood between the two girls. His frame disappeared under Dynasty's five feet six inch tall shadow. "Sorry Dynasty."

"Excuse me. Am I invisible or are you blind?" Macy's hands rested on her hips.

"Macy, you talk too much. But yea excuse me."

"You're excused." She responded sarcastically.

Cupping the ball under his arm and to the side Aaron turned to Dynasty. "So who are you going to the dance with?"

"Why are you asking?"

"Just asking." He shied away.

Macy couldn't wait to jump into the conversation. "His musty behind wants to take you."

"You talk too much Macy, that's why I know you don't have a date. You wish my musty behind was taking you."

"Well let me crack some egg on your pie face. We're all are going as a group. No guys, just the girls. So technically I do have a date and you don't. Right Dy?"

"She has a mouth. Let her answer. Why don't you go over there and watch them play so we can talk in private?" Aaron suggested while pointing towards the other boys that stood waiting for the ball to finish the game. "Take this with you."

Dynasty hesitated. He had her rethinking their plans. Aaron was the most popular boy at the high school. He made her nervous because there were rumors that he was just out for sex and once he got a girl the whole school knew about it. Sadly, she secretly had been hoping that he would ask, the classic good girl liking the bad guy scenario. They could be the Prince and Princess of the dance. At least that's how she played it out in her mind. "I don't have a date and Macy's right. I think we have plenty of time for all that. Like junior, senior prom."

Aaron worked hard to hide his disappointment. "You thinking ahead, huh?"

"You can call it that. That's if you're still single. You know your reputation is pretty uh…" She didn't want to say what everybody else was saying nor did she want to scare him off."

"Still single?

"You think I got it like that?"

"I know you got it like that."

"Why don't I have a date then?" The degrees of separation were getting smaller. Aaron was totally violating the personal space rule but she didn't mind. "And what about my reputation? Seem like you know more about me than me?"

Dynasty felt the butterflies in her stomach and her voice showed her nervousness. "I don't know much. Just heard a few things." Biting her lip she couldn't bring herself to say the things she heard. She knew all about sex, babies, and a little more but it still felt uncomfortable saying it to him. Those kinds of conversations were reserved for the girl talk.

"I'm all ears." Curiosity got the best of him and wouldn't allow him to let it go. A mischievous grin came across his face as he stepped so close that he bumped her.

"Personal space violation. Get on back! And if you must know let's just say that you are probably a little more advanced than I am. But that's your business just don't hope you become a teen dad. That's not a good look."

"Ouch. You don't hold no punches do you."

"Calling like it is but back to that original question. We have time- maybe junior prom? Senior prom? Maybe?"

"Maybe." Revealing as many teeth as possible he smiled and bumped up against her again.

"And after a bath."

"You're tough."

"I hear that a lot." The streetlight flickered bouncing perfectly off Dynasty's copper colored eyes. "We all know what that mean." The flutter of her eyelashes outpaced her moving lips as Dynasty brought the evening fun to a close. The streets of Hawthorne Trace emptied quickly. "Macy. Come on girl."

***

"Dynasty I see you're wearing a little more makeup than we agreed upon. How many times do I have to say you are pretty enough without all that extra. I'm starting not to recognize you and I don't like that."

"Momma, it is not that bad. Come on now. I wanted to see how the new Wet and Wild products looked on me before the dance."

"Wet and wild exactly." Doris let out a boisterous laugh and Dynasty soon joined. "It looks very pretty but as I always say you don't need too much. Stay my sweet 16 a little longer, will you ma'am."

"I'm growing up. I will stay sweet but can't promise you 16."

"I love your sense of humor. Always looking on the brighter side of things."

"I get that from you. No bad days. Right?

"You are right."

Finding a spot to sit at the foot of the bed Dynasty propped her mom's feet on her lap. The television was the only audible sound in the room while Dynasty's fingers kneaded the sole's of the feet that had walked all day on the third floor maternity unit of Mercy General. Doris had found herself pregnant at 40 and widowed shortly after. Being a nurse provided a decent living for Dynasty and herself but the hours were long and sometimes hard. She worried about spending enough time with Dynasty, but she was sure to keep her busy, and make every game, cheering the loudest from the stands.

"That feels real good baby. Thank you for doing that. Even when I don't ask."

"Doris Langston, my only mother, you take such good care of everybody. All those momma's and their babies, day in and day out-- the least I can do is take care of you."

"Dynasty Langston, you are one of a kind and I'm so glad you're mine." The doting on one another was all too familiar. "You will be the belle of the dance and I'm happy with your dress choice. I was getting a little worried."

"Worried? You know I was going to keep it classy with just a little bit of sassy."

"That's what worried me." She winked. "There is so much going on nowadays and everybody wants to grow up so fast. Getting into all kind of trouble. The mommas are getting younger and younger over there."

"Yes momma. But that's not me. Trust me and know I will always do the right thing." Dynasty felt a little guilt. She was thinking about Aaron and wished she had let him walk her home. He was quite the cutie and interested in her. She was interested in him as well but no dating was allowed right now they would revisit the conversation when she turned 17.

"Yes, I know. I guess that's what moms do. When you are grown and married with children of your own you'll get it. Until then stay my beautiful, sweet 16 year old."

"Ummmm. I can promise you beautiful and sweet but I can't promise you 16."

When No One Came

"I'll take it." Oh I almost forgot I will be pulling a double next Friday so I will be a little late getting you after the dance. But I should be there by 10:30."

"That means no I can't catch a ride with so and so even though their mom said it was okay."

"You beat me to it! Just when I thought you weren't paying any attention."

"I listen momma. Well about 90% of the time."

"90% huh? What am I going to do with you?" Doris asked shaking her head. "Dinner's ready. Go fix your plate before the food gets cold."

"Oh and can you ask Mrs. Smith if she would let me do Macy's makeup for the dance."

"Child now you know good and well Diane is not going for that."

"That's your girl. She listens to you."

"That is my girl but Macy is hers. We'll see.

"Ok, I'm going to go over after school on Thursday and you can ask then when you pick me up." Dynasty laid out the plan.

"You two are always plotting. Well thank you for telling me instead of asking."

"Now go eat. Please."

"Yes ma'am. Sorry about that. Will you pick me up and may I go over after school."

"Yes Dynasty, you may go."

Leaning in front of Doris to offer a kiss, "There are no bogeymen in little old Merriweather County, South Carolina momma but if you insist. I will wait but please don't make me wait too long."

"I promise."

INTRODUCING THE HAWKS

"Spring has sprung." Tressa's long coffee toned legs peered from under her dress. A stonewashed denim jacket completed the ensemble and provided just enough of a barrier against the chill. Although the sun was dancing across the sky the newness of spring was still settling in. The trees were just beginning to leaf out and nights were still cool. "This may be my favorite seasons out of the two."

"Two?"

Tressa laughed. "You know the running joke. Nevada has two seasons, warm and hot. Spring is here and I'm here for it."

"Hold your horses. It hasn't sprung quite yet. It's about 65 degrees and that's still chilly." Olivia countered. "I've been here all my life and still laugh at how it seems we bypass a real spring season every year and I've never heard that running joke but it makes sense. Where is the other Radcliffe?"

"Fashionably late as always Warden Thibodeaux." They laughed.

"One thing for sure Marissa will take an hour to style that

afro- pick it, shape it , shine it and then pick, shape and shine some more. I'm thankful for my maintenance free do." Tressa winked as her hands caressed her freshly cut natural fade.

Olivia paused and smiled. "Beauty is her name." Tressa's high cheekbones and thin nose were accentuated with the perfect contour of bronze makeup. Her oval face complimented her close natural haircut. In her other life she could have been a high fashion model.

"Thanks doll. Now only if Mr. Right can see this same beauty." A deflated sigh emphasized the sarcasm in her voice.

"In due time my dear. I'm hopeful romantic after all. Other than that how have you been? How has business been doing?" The ladies had not been able to keep up with each for a while. After college Olivia decided to move back to her home state and the other ladies followed, deciding on Carson City, the state's capital. It was a small family oriented city where most couples had 1 or no children. The city was rich in history and actually home to a few Native American tribes. It wasn't too bad for travel either. Action was all around- gambling, girls nearby or big city living and dreaming across the way in California. All in all the ladies thought they had chosen a nice place to settle for the time being.

"You know O; I'm in a good space right now. I'm happy that I didn't pick up and move with Mark. He hates Houston. Complains about the traffic every time we talk. He's dating again and I'm okay with that. Glad he told me but I figured it wouldn't be long."

"That negro, with his needy behind."

"Yes ma'am so I knew it wouldn't be long. Business is great. I was actually thinking about opening a second location.

It's easy when you don't have much competition and folks will always need a dentist."

"Do it. I'm refer my clients to you every chance I get. One thing about being a stylist somebody will ask you for a referral for almost anything. And it's a place where people talk and share information. Sometimes too much information." They giggled.

"I appreciate that Olivia. Now your turn. What's going on in O's world?"

"Ain't nothing going on but the rent, perms, weaves, and gossip."

"That sounds like something, not nothing."

"Ha, If you want to call it that. Seriously, I can't complain. Solid clientele, struggling to get these few added pounds off now since I *am* dating again. I miss hanging with y'all. But all in all, the usual."

"Back up. I see how you just glossed over that dating again. Ahem. I'm listening."

"Not much to it. Met him at the grocery store. We've been seeing each other for a few months. He's divorced with kids so holding off on introducing him. I need a few more months to make sure his ex- wife isn't messy. That usually doesn't come out until after the new lady meets the kids."

"True."

"We'll see. I just know somebody needs to get hitched so we can have some more babies around here."

"Hello divas!" Tressa and Olivia turned to see Gay and

Marissa strolling across the patio towards them dressed like polar opposites. Gay's one piece hugged every inch of her body. Black granny boots with a chunky heel were the perfect pairing. Marissa jumped straight to the hot weather wearing a pair of hot pick hot shorts, and a tank top with a long sleeve denim shirt. The shirt was longer than the shorts.

"Gay where are your manners?" Olivia's mother hen personality turned on.

Lowering her shades to show her eyes Gay smirked, "We're outside therefore no inside voice is needed, now gimme love."

"You are something else lady. Anyhoo, hello to you two forever late divas."

"Ahem." Tressa interjected. "While the three of you play kissy face I'm headed to the ladies room and will one of you gals order me another mimosa. I'll give my love when I get back."

"Please excuse our tardiness there was an accident on Grover and Boulevard so we had to take the long way around. Then we stopped at a boutique on the way and…"

"Save it. Just rude. But it's all good. You called the meeting. You're late, so you are paying the tab. Drink up everybody."

"I got it." Gay smiled patting her purse.

Taking a minute to soak up the scenery and a little sun, the ladies sipped mimosas and sat. The Blue Lagoon was a new addition to downtown Carson City. Nestled on the corner of the strip mall, its location was perfect. Anyone that was caught by the traffic light couldn't help but see it. The outside was just okay, nothing too fancy that would strike a person's curiosity besides it being new and the sidewalk sign that read bottomless mimosas. The inside and outside were in stark contrast to one another. Decorative art and original paintings covered the walls. The ceilings were painted a bright orange and complemented the red and orange furniture perfectly. Water flowed from three fountains on the patio. A wall fountain covered the entire side of the building.

"This place is stunning." Tressa couldn't help but notice. "Maybe we can start back having our monthly brunches here."

The other ladies nodded and chimed in agreement. "Yes it is. Absolutely. Sounds good to me."

Resting her shades on top of her head, "Well the hour has come." Gay called their attention. "I asked you ladies, my sisters to join me at brunch to discuss something very important. Something very urgent." She paused to gather her thoughts.

Simultaneously the ladies placed their glasses on the table. When Gay the hardly ever-serious one said it was serious or important, they listened. Tressa cut her eyes to Marissa for a quick clue. If anyone knew what was going on Marissa did. And if she did she held it close to her.

"As you all know I've been running GT Investigations solo for three years now. Things have been really good. I mean really good. Good enough to hire an assistant and a part time person. I'm still wondering what the hell I'm paying her for." Shaking her head she continued. "But that's another story for another time."

The women looked at Gay eagerly, their eyes saying 'come on with it'.

"Lately, I've been receiving calls that have been asking for help atypical of what the firm is used to doing. Cheating husband- check. Cheating wife- check. Employee lying about injury- check. Tracking down lost money and the person behind it- check. Finding paper trails, finding accounts, cars, and houses. You all know the drill-- money and people, we find," Gay puffed and rightfully so. Her biggest haul was a 10 million dollar investment scheme. She tracked the broker all the way to Hong Kong and was able to recover every dime with interest. That had to be the tipping point that catapulted her into a semi spotlight or at least name recognition.

"Yes and we are definitely proud of you. Although we thought you were crazy when you said you were leaving the psychology field. Who knew it would be a stupid smart?" Olivia gave semi props. "Talk about an oxymoron."

They all laughed.

"I also wondered if it was a smart move considering you had baby girl to take care of. Who would leave a definite paycheck and benefits for a dream?" Olivia continued. "Not many. That safety net can get real comfortable."

"A dreamer." Tressa answered. "I'm glad you did. You made it work."

"Okay, can I finish?" Gay laughed while dabbing at her eyes. "Y'all getting all mushy on me and shit. In all seriousness I do appreciate your support and being there for me through the slow start up times. It was a bit difficult. I knew explaining to my parents why I needed to come home would be impossible even though that degree I decided not use didn't cost them a thing."

"So you've been getting calls?" Marissa brought the conversation back to focus.

"Yes, I've only received a few but a few too many asking if I find missing children."

"Missing as in runaway? Kidnapped?" Tressa moved to the edge of her seat.

"Both I guess. I really didn't ask too many questions. Told them their local law officials were better equipped for that and since I'm not legally able to enforce the law or anything like it I would be in over my head. But this last call has really been on my mind. There's a couple in Florida that have been looking for their daughter for almost two years now. She was 10 at the time she went missing in the summer of 1998. The same age as Naja."

"Wow. So she's almost twelve and still hasn't been found? I never heard about a girl being kidnapped in Florida. Then again do these kidnappings ever make national news?" This barrage of questions was followed by silence. The ladies waited for more information.

"Not really. Local coverage and depending how much noise is made, the national media may pick it up and run a story here or there. Anyway that has been sitting with me. Weighing on me heavily."

Marissa had been privy to this information because she and Gay were the closest. Suggesting that she share what had been transpiring with the others; Marissa hoped collectively they could help Gay find a solution or peace in making a decision to help or to not help.

Beseeching her friends Gay asked for feedback, "What are you all thinking? The mom has called me three times asking me to reconsider. I promised I would give her an answer either way by the weekend. It's really no pressure."

"How could you not help?" Olivia asked

"Never said I wouldn't. I just don't think it's that simple. That cut and dry."

Pushing her to really dissect the issue. Olivia chose to ask all the right questions. "What's different besides the age of the missing person? You said yourself you know how to find people. That's what you do."

"If only it were that simple. We are looking at time, resources, moving away from my comfort zone, being intimately connected with families that are looking for a loved one. I would be looking for a child who is young and innocent; someone that wouldn't know how to be found even if they wanted to. Not some grown man or woman who could give a damn if they broke up a happy home or if they ripped someone off. Grown people who have 100 percent control over their actions. It's quite different."

"Yeah, I get that it may be hard. I still think you should help. What do you need us to do? What do you want us to do?" Olivia insisted.

"I need your help. I'm not asking you to quit your jobs or anything but take some time to come along with me. Help me research and fact find. Help me make some calls and knock on a few doors. I'm not sure what it will take right now but I do know it will take more than me."

"I'm in without a doubt. " Marissa raised her hand followed by Olivia. Tressa hesitated and then raised her hand at the moment to not be the lone one. She didn't want to feel like she wasn't down for her lifetime friends, but she also wanted more time to really consider what was being asked. If the phone calls, research, and whatever other tasks were completed led to something substantial, what would be the next thing? Were they going to turn that information over to the police or were they going in for a rescue?

"You be hawking girl." Tressa pretended to be all in. "I don't know if we are as good as you but we can give it a go."

Gay smiled. "I take that as a compliment. You all don't have to be as good just yet... but you will be. It's a necessity. Hawking huh?"

"Yep."

"We can't form a group without a name now. What gang do you know that doesn't have a name?" Marissa popped her neck with sass. "Am I right or am I right?"

"Leave it to my ghetto sister to come up with that. You are wrong on so many levels. First of all we ain't banging. No gang affiliation hun. You momma and daddy raised you better."

"Our momma and daddy ma'am. Gay what say you? This is your thing. It's too many of us to be on some old Cagney and Lacey tip."

"Hilarious. What did you say Tressa? I be hawking?"

"Yeah. We all gonna be hawking. The Hawks? How does that sound?

Tressa mustered a nervous smile. "I like." She knew she needed to support her friend and didn't want to be the lone wolf but she couldn't help but be apprehensive about getting into something she didn't know much about.

"I can dig it." Marissa was excited and even happier that they could support Gay. "What's next?"

"Glad you asked." I need to call Mrs. Mabrey back and let her know I will take the case. We got some work to do on our end to get ready, but the action needs to be swift. Two years is a long time for any parent to wonder where their child is."

ADVANCED TRAINING

The seatbelts were no match against the rugged terrain. The ladies bounced up and down in their seats as the Jeep Wrangler made its way down the winding gravel path, jostling them from side to side. The speed over the gravel stirred up a trail of dust that lingered behind. The off road capability of the tires added very little comfort because Gay was showing no mercy on the drive. They were one rollover away from a serious accident. It had been two months since the ladies formally organized the Hawks. Gay was proficient in what she did and although the ladies had the sixth sense or intuition that most women did, that intuition and ability to connect the dots really didn't go beyond snooping and uncovering things on their own turf. It was much easier to navigate personal, familiar spaces than the unknown. The desert sun beat down on their heads and the dust left their mouths dry and cottony.

"Are we there yet?" Olivia was miserable and felt sick from motion sickness.

Sweat saturated the double-layered tanks Tressa wore. "You know this is cruel and unusual right? I didn't sign up for this," her voice competing with the open air and blaring radio.

"We are almost there." Gay took her eyes off of the road briefly turning to answer Olivia.

The warm water wasn't satisfying but it was hydrating. "You owe us big time." Tressa gulped pouring more water on her than drinking.

"Come on now. We can't take down the bad guys without the right skills and knowing how to use the tools properly."

"I knew there was more to it, calling folk, knocking on doors, and some researching. Wasn't that the gist you gave?"

"Pretty much." Gay turned again.

"Ok, keep your eyes on the road. I'm not trying to have a shoot out or be doing some all out street fighting with anybody. I'll save that for the movies." Tressa laughed. "But I will kick somebody's ass if I need to."

"See, you all over the place. One minute you all scary and the next you a baddy. In all seriousness, this is basic self-defense, and goes with the territory. Any woman should know this, law enforcement or not. Private investigations or not, a woman should know how to protect herself if ever in harm's way. It's some psychos out here."

"I get it, but we didn't have to come out here for that. You know that little lovely gym we all belong to? They do offer self defense classes."

Gay tried to contain herself. She knew this was going to be good. This rude awakening was going to be something to remember. She had asked the trainers to go hard. "Yeah I know."

Pulling into an old aircraft hangar Gay gave a vote of confidence while pleading her case to spending a day and a half in the middle of nowhere. Technically it wasn't the middle of nowhere but an abandoned airport that once flew small private planes. The terrain to get there was rugged only because Gay had decided to take the back road. The women sat for a few minutes to regain their composure and to breathe in dust free air.

"We've been waiting on you." Their rest was interrupted by a strange voice walking towards the jeep. Extending a hand, a burly 6 feet 4ish man greeted them. The women sat in the jeep and turned to look at him before resuming their resting state. "How was the drive?" He continued to try and engage them.

"Gay, get your friend." Marissa swiped her hand towards her. "Let us catch our breath while you handle whatever business with Mr. Rambo."

"Oh! We all have business with Mr. Rambo so rest up for another 5 minutes. Then come on."

Five minutes turned into 15, but Gay allowed them that because she knew the fellas were going to bring the pain. They all stood in a line as the strange man and his partner walked down and greeted each of them. "Go on and put your bags down. We have lots of ground to cover." A formal introduction was still lacking.

"And where she we put our bags?" Tressa looked around seeing no building that remotely resembled a hotel or place to lodge.

"Awww Gay didn't tell you I see?"

"Tell?" Cutting her eyes towards Gay."

"We camp out up here. No concierge, fancy bellhops, or room service in these parts. Just us and nature."

"Yeah right? The nights are still cold and we're black

women. We don't camp out. Didn't you get the memo?"

"That's the best excuse I've heard in a long time. But I'm sure you all will make it work. Now the memo that I did get is that women are quite resilient and resourceful especially when options are few."

Tressa thought to herself. Excuse hell. Who was crazy enough to be camping out in the middle of no damn where with two white men that looked like they were on steroids? "Gay! Really? What's the deal? You said nothing about camping out. Only pack enough clothes for two days."

"Calm down. It's going to be fine. John and Mike are the best at what they do and come with high recommendations and commendations." She pretended that this would be her first time working with them as well.

"And exactly what do they do? Eat people for a living?" Marissa chimed in.

"You ladies are quite the comedians and just may be our toughest bunch yet." Mike interjected while trying to hide his smile. "Let's start over. My name is Mike Rosebaum and John Leblanc here is my partner. We have over 35 combined years of experience in tactical training and self defense." His arms flexed under the two sizes too small tee shirt. The fatigues and military style boots were quite intimidating. "We have a one and a half day crash course as we understand you will be deploying on a mission soon."

"Deploying?" Marissa was growing antsy. "We are not in the military so you don't have to use that lingo. Got me feeling like I'm in boot camp or something. I decided a long time ago that manual labor or anything too strenuous was not for me."

When No One Came

"Now, now ladies. Calm down. Damn! Y'all giving me a headache. Thanks Olivia for not giving them a hard time."

"I guess. I was just about to crank it up."

"We're in good hands. And don't worry I'm sure they're good at pitching tents and lighting fires. They were scouts before they were SEAL." Gay attempted to ease the tension with a little humor.

"I think we remember how. Once a scout always a scout." John finally spoke.

"But we are definitely better at putting the fires out. All jokes aside, on the backside of the hangar are your sleeping quarters. Take your bags around there, choose your tent, and let's use the rest of this daylight for getting down to business." Mike insisted.

***

The women were not dressed properly for the training although they brought all the items suggested by Mike and John via Gay. The dust had settled and the sun was going down which made the conditions more tolerable for June, one of the hottest months of the summer for Nevada. In all the years that the ladies had resided in Carson City, they never really took the time to do the tourist thing or explore outside of the city. All outings were usually business and semi pleasure that took them to another state for the most part. The landscape was breathtakingly beautiful. Rows and rows of mountains and hills could be seen in the distance. Dry earth unexpectedly met patches of grass. The land was not completely barren. Cacti and grass showed signs of life. A halo of orange and red surrounded the setting sun. It was peaceful. Once the ladies let their frustrations go, they were able to see the beauty of nature. Even more important, the beauty of stillness and quiet, and how critical it would be for what was ahead.

"Let's do a few stretches. Right hand extended over left shoulder and pull." John led the session. This was pretty easy for the ladies as they all were similarly athletically inclined. Marissa and Tressa both attended UCLA on a track scholarship, Olivia and Gay played basketball. They had managed to continue be physically active after their college years. "Now to the other side."

"Gay?" Tressa was still giving her the blues.

"Drop and give me 50 pushups then 50 jump- squats followed by 5 sets of lunges. The name of the game is no whining. Let me be clear- whining adds 10 more of everything and it doesn't matter who it comes from."

They pushed through the pain, gritted their teeth and saw it through. It wasn't as though they weren't familiar with boot camp style exercising. Having been off their regular exercise schedule had thrown a monkey wrench in their endurance and stamina, which felt like next to nothing.

Mike offered water. "Drink as much as you need. You're probably dried out from the sun and the long ride up here. It will help you get through so just holler if you need to hydrate."

The ladies pushed through the sets and got water at the end. Not knowing if they should be mad or happy about the training, they didn't say a word, but waited to be instructed on the next step. The upside was that they were acquiring some useful skills and knowledge that all women should know. That was not complaint worthy. It didn't hurt that the disclaimer had been made about whining.

When No One Came

"Ok ladies, we're going to go through a series of tactical maneuvers that will teach you how to take an assailant down. Or anyone that needs to be taken down. This is usually true for those violating your personal space. Say you're out shopping and some perp tries to rob you or sexually assault you. Let's say someone is on to you and confronts you about taking pictures and following them. It could be any number of things that make you feel uncomfortable and unsafe. Let's hope that never happens but with your line of work. It probably will, to varying degrees."

This was one added thing that gave Olivia even more pause. She let out a sigh and waited for the next set of instructions. A headache was coming on.

"Know we are not trying to scare you or intimidate you. Just putting everything out there." assured John. "Pair up and I will work with two of you and Mike will work with the other two. Let's move to the grassy area to soften any falls."

Gay and Olivia paired up and Tressa and Marissa joined each other. This was the perfect combination because they weren't equal in weight and height much like an assailant would be.

"Turn your back to your partner. Partners come up behind and grab the victims around the neck or waist. Victims move forward and then backwards. The goal is to throw the perp off balance with that movement. If the person is taller it would probably flip them over your shoulder depending on the amount of force used."

This training went on for a couple of hours. The ladies went over everything, from front facing attacks to attacks with weapons and those without. It seemed like John and Mike covered every scenario possible. He made them unlearn what they thought they knew. The brain is the most powerful weapon a person could use when protecting themselves. The men gave the example of a horror movie. Time and time again the victim ends up running and falling or running straight to the attacker when they could have very well run to the car grabbed the spare key and gotten away.

"You ladies are probably on brain overload right now I'm sure." John asked while secretly winking at Gay.

"No way. I can do this for another four-five hours." Marissa couldn't help herself. Speaking from half delirium and half fatigue.

It was pitch black. A few high-powered flashlights added to the light from the night sky. "Ok- cry uncle and you can go." Although the ladies were tired and emotions ran high they knew crying uncle meant giving up or accepting defeat and that was not going to happen.

"Not happening. Yeah you kicked our ass but that's not happening."

"Marissa you are one tough cookie. And on that note good night." John excused them.

They still didn't speak overwhelmed with emotions. Not in the sense that they were angry or upset but their nerves were unsettled. They didn't know what to expect and weren't quite sure if they were ready or would ever be ready. One thing that they all came to terms with in their own minds was that a child needed them and they couldn't turn back now. It was a life or death situation.

LOCKED AND LOADED

The sun had barely peeked over the hills. Just a glimmer of light could be seen from inside the tent. The fire was still going and had kept them warm throughout the night. The coyote or rattlesnake they were dreading never came to greet them. Any slight movement hurt. They hurt badly. Muscle fatigue and soreness was almost intolerable, enough to make them whine and cry if they dwelled on it too long.

A loud squeal from a whistle signaled that it was time to get up and get the day started. After about three blows the ladies stumbled out of their tents slowly mumbling to themselves all kinds of obscenities while squinting from the sun.

"Good morning beauties." John smiled. "You have 45 minutes to shower, dress, and get some chow. You can eat what you brought or one of our ready to eat meals. I suggest you rub down with this. I'm sure you could use it." He handing them each a tub of muscle rub. The tube read greaseless, deep penetrating pain relief. Hours of relief from minor arthritis, backache, muscle & joint pain.

"You do have a heart?" Tressa exclaimed with just a tad of

sarcasm. "Never got this in boot camp before.

"Boot camp? You really think that's what this is?"

"Feels like it."

"Nope. It's called survival. That's a necessity in any situation. I know you watch the news. You have heard and seen the stories. We are living in far more dangerous times. So you must know what it takes. We're out in the desert. You don't have the luxuries as in the city, in your home, or office. So you have to improvise and make it work. Where you all are headed, you need to know how to survive in the toughest situations." John was serious about his business and didn't sugar coat the seriousness of the Hawks' business.

"You are absolutely right..." her voice trailed off as she walked to the shower. In her mind she wondered if there was something that Gay wasn't telling them. The sense of urgency John spoke with was frightening. Maybe she was over thinking it. His job was to teach people how to survive. Maybe it was so ingrained in him that it became the only language that he knew how to speak.

"How are you all feeling? What are you thinking?" Gay was concerned. She knew this would be put her in the hot seat but didn't bother her. She was used to being in the hot seat. Although she hadn't dealt with any real serious or dangerous situations, she did have a few confrontations and the only weapon she used was a stun gun and some mace. Even though she knew that unless these items were in clear view and ready to use, being stuck in a purse was a lost cause. An attacker would be on you in a split second and you're still digging for mace. These two self-defense tools just sat better than a gun. "Be honest. Now is the time."

When No One Came

Marissa was the first to speak. "Honest? When have we ever not been?" I'm fine. It's a bit much to take in and everything seems to be moving fast. But I get it. Time is of the essence. It's already been too long for Josalyn."

"Are you really fine?" Gay sensed otherwise having known her for the last 20 years. Having known all them for the last 20 years.

"Yes I am and you know I would tell you if it were anything more."

"Thank you friend."

"For? No thank you for caring and being so brave. I still need to tell Jonathan all the details. That man is going to kill me. Now rub some of that bravery off on me." Rubbing Gay's shoulder she let out a nervous giggle. She had shared bits and pieces of what was going on and had intended to divulge everything but let time and the right opportunity get away. Now she had signed up for the team and was in the middle of advanced training; definitely not a good look for a married woman.

"I'm good. I understand your passion or need to do this somewhat. Still wrapping my head around what we are attempting to do and how it could all play out. I see the love you speak about between parent and child daily as the parents comfort and support their little ones through routine dental care. Even the teenagers have someone there supporting them, if not just to bring them in for the visit. I see that love with you and Naja. For that matter the love my parents have for us even as adults. So I get the empathy. Just… still wrapping my mind around *if* we should be doing this." Tressa gave a candid response. One that was open, honest, and raw. Her uncertainty and apprehension could not be denied.

"I appreciate you and that." acknowledging Tressa, Gay, coming from her usual stoic space, winked at her. "And you're right. It doesn't have to be us. It could be any of the thousand of investigators out there. It could be the police who get paid to do this thing everyday. It could be the neighborhood watch. It could very well be anybody but us. But the truth of the matter is I got the call, more than once. There can be no mistake in that. Truthfully, I don't think I could live with myself if I didn't at least try. If you heard the anguish in that woman's voice, I'm willing to bet everything I own that you would at least give it a try if given the chance."

Olivia was the last to speak. Her voice was not the usual strong and feisty sound everyone knew. She spoke low from a worn out place. Tressa had said exactly what she wanted to say. Everything. "That's a good sell chica. I can't lie. I'm nervous as hell. I don't want to interrupt my life, my client's life, and my normal routine trying to save the world. Well that may be an exaggeration. But you get what I'm saying"

"You think?" Marissa laughed attempting to lighten the heavy conversation before the sound of the whistle cut through. Her phone rang. They had agreed to keep the phones on in case of emergencies but anything else would have to wait until they got back down to the city. Jonathan was not an emergency but she knew she needed to take it. Instead she sent him to a voicemail followed by a quick text that read, TTYL. She could only imagine what her husband was thinking. If the shoe was on the other foot she knew what she would think.

***

"Hey guys. You have a sec?"

"Sure Gay, what's up?" Mike asked.

"I know we had a few more things on the schedule. Let's table it for now. Still bill me at full rate because I believe in paying people for their time. I just think we need to finish it later."

"What's wrong?"

"Can't say that anything is wrong per se. I just think I moved them too fast. It's a bit overwhelming and I sense it. We are all tired. I think after this session we're gonna head on back down. I could use some sleep, a real long hot shower, and my bed."

"You're spot on. I could sense something different this morning also. I probably caused some of the angst as well. Implying that they may be in a really dangerous situation and need to know how to protect themselves."

"I think it's more. But will get to the heart of it later."

"This session is very dangerous. I'm going to advise against having inexperienced women shooting. Especially tired inexperienced women. But it's your call and theirs at the end of the day."

"I think it will be fine. I'm sure at this juncture if I give the option 1 or 2 may say let's roll. Let's get a few rounds in and we will meet up again in a few weeks."

"Deal?"

"If you are okay with it. So I am I? Mike patted her on the shoulder. "You got a tough team. It's solid even though it may appear shaky. It doesn't get any better than working with folk who genuinely like you and have your best interest at heart. Those kinds of people will not only be looking out for themselves but you as well. They're more apt to make better choices keeping you and themselves out of harm's way."

"I think so too. These are my warriors."

"Once the nerves are gone. Y'all are gonna be one hell of a force to reckon with. You already a force by yourself Gay." John bragged.

The four rows of target stands were approximately 3 feet apart. On each stand were protective eyewear, earplugs and a black 9-millimeter Glock pistol, a .45 Automatic Colt pistol and a .380 Automatic Colt pistol, the latter two being more for personal protection use. They were small and concealable. A sandbag rested at the foot of each stand. Straight ahead were black silhouette targets on white paper. The high retaining wall was in place to stop the bullets. The scene was something right out of a movie.

"Take a few minutes to inspect everything at your station. Remember safety first. Follow the steps we discussed this morning." John stood on one end and Mike on the other. Today their demeanor was softened. The drill sergeant persona was gone, Gay stepping aside and speaking with them before the morning session must have had something to do with it. The ladies noticed and mentioned this amongst themselves.

"Okay Hawks. Take your positions by the stand; get your glasses on and your earplugs ready. The first few shots will be test shots. That means shoot straight ahead not necessarily at the target but to get the feel of the gun in your hand and then the feel of shooting that same gun. We'll go through shooting all three guns. Get your ear plugs." Mike leading the session gave careful instruction.

Having gone over the parts of the gun, how to hold it and other background safety issues of using these types of guns earlier, the ladies took their positions and prepared to take turns firing three rounds each from each of them. Shooting in the air and not at something was easy.

"That was good. Now let's use the targets. We want to aim at the center of the body. Let's start by holding the gun in the firing ready position. If you are not shooting your gun should be downwards facing, safety on and hand off the trigger."

The cool air didn't prevent the women from sweating; from beads of sweat on the forehead to sweat stains under the arms. Their nervousness could not be hidden. None of them owned a gun with the exception of Gay. None of them considered owning a gun either. The security guards at work, their cell phones on ready, and the alarms at work gave them a false sense of security.

"Gay since you've had the training and are already licensed to carry a gun why don't you start?" It made sense. She also wanted to show the others that it was really not much to it.

Nodding she raised and extended her arms up in the firing ready position. Her feet were hip width apart. Leaning forward just a tad to counteract the gun's recoil she gripped the gun as tight as she could.

"Ready, aim, shoot." Mike paused. "Ready, aim, shoot." He paused again. "Ready, aim, shoot." The sound of the Glock pierced the air. A few birds could be seen scattering in the distance. The sun was rising to its noon position, beating down and shining bright, suffocating the cool breeze that seemed to be blowing only a few minutes earlier.

Gay fired 3 more rounds in the direction of the target unflinching with a different gun. From her vantage point it appeared her shots were dead center. Not that it mattered. They all knew being put in a real life situation it could go anyway. She prayed that if it ever were the case the situation would favor her.

"Marissa, you're next. Ready?"

"Ready as I ever will be." Psyching herself up, she raised the gun up to the firing position and nodded.

"Ready, aim, shoot."

She squeezed the trigger of the .35 and the hammer flew back and it caught the skin between her finger and thumb. A quick reflex caused her to drop the gun. "Shit." The other ladies ran to her attention.

"Get back to your stands. We talked about this. Rushing and not taking your time will cause this. I knew you were going to get pinched just by the grip."

"Well why didn't you say something." Marissa asked while he poured some cold water on it. I didn't hurt too badly. She was more embarrassed that she had flubbed her first round.

"Everybody look at me... again." Mike stood in front to demonstrate. "This is not what you want to do prior to firing a weapon." He held a dummy gun up in the firing ready position and squeezed the trigger. "Notice how lazy my grip was and my position was off. We want to palm the side of the gun and the handle where it's flush against our hand."

"Like this." John stepped beside Marissa and handed her the gun while assisting her with placement. "Now how does that feel?"

"It's ok." Trying to ignore the redness and sting from the pinch.

"What does ok mean?"

"It means ok. It feels snug in my hand. I have a tight grip. Look at my knuckles."

"Yeah that's too tight. No white knuckles and no trembling hands." John pulled at her hands a little to loosen the grip.

"Now how does that feel?"

"Better."

"Ready?"

"As ever," she replied.

Mike sounded off again. "Ready, aim, shoot." This time she emptied the clip, laid the gun back on the stand, stood upright and didn't say a word.

"Nice."

"I hear ya. But why didn't you correct me the first time?

"Much like a child. We tell them the stove is hot and as soon as you turn your head they have to get a feel of the heat themselves. Not saying you are a child but that's the perfect analogy to us going over the books, going over the guns and the proper way to hold them and shoot, and yet you grab it and go totally skipping over the proper set-up."

"You got me."

"No harm, really. Just a little pinch and no foul. You came back and perfectly executed." He was sure to keep her confidence in tact.

"Tressa. You're up next.

"Looks like it." Her voice shook.

"You say when and I will call." Mike gave her space. "Your call."

After what seemed like eternity. She nodded and raised the gun to the firing position.

"Ready, aim, shoot." Mike instructed. Tressa didn't pull the trigger. "Ready, aim, shoot." He instructed again a little louder assuming she didn't hear him the first time. Nothing.

"I can't do this. I'm not trying to kill anyone or be in a situation that I need to kill someone." All along Olivia thought she would be the first one to crack.

STAKEOUT #2

Not much had been said about the incident at the range. Everyone thought it best to let it stay there and delegate accordingly. For now, Tressa was on desk duty instead of doing fieldwork that involved the Florida case or any new missing child case. This is where she felt most comfortable and Gay was okay with that. Particularly since she didn't have to be involved at all.

"Olivia my dear, make sure you take better pictures this time. Please and thank you."

"It's not me it's this million dollar camera you bought. Seriously Gay, rocket science has to be easier to navigate. Keep in mind I'm a hairstylist by trade. Not Carrie Mae Weems or Simpson." These two women photographed everything from high fashion to politics, anything that sought to tear down the limits of the black experience.

"Well it sounds like you know a little something about

photography."

"I do. I see it. I like it. I buy it from prints to high-end portraits. That's about it and lot simpler than trying to capture what I'm not an expert in."

"Geez Louise. No lecture needed. I got it. Just remind me to remind you to read the manual. No study the manual."

"Jokey jokes, huh?"

The Hawks made a few more executive decisions over the course of the month. In addition to roles, they also decided that it would be best to split the work on surveillance and answering after hours calls. This lessened the interruptions of their work schedules in the day although Tressa and Olivia decided to take an additional day off to work in the office. Clearly an added benefit of being self employed.

"I guess you get a pass." Gay winked. "How are you feeling? Nerves better?

"I guess you could say that. I do appreciate day surveillance though. It's so much better. You can actually see some stuff."

"Stuff like?"

"The perps. Can't nobody creep up on you." She was still slightly stuck on the whole tactical maneuver/advanced training quasi boot camp.

"I agree. It's definitely better for visibility but riskier because we can get busted. Real quick. Just like we can see them. You better believe they can see us."

"But they would have to know we are there first which seems highly unlikely."

"You gotta a point. We'll roll with it as needed and see how it works out."

***

A phone conversation from earlier in the week and a call from the wife revealed Mr. CEO would be traveling to Los Angeles for a business conference. It also revealed he wouldn't be traveling alone. Gay and Marissa flew to LA at her request. What had been discovered to date was already enough for her to easily have a judgment in her favor, but she was out for blood. No cost was too high or distance too far to make sure every t was crossed and i dotted. Gay also suspected that the status of the other woman fueled the wife's persistence.

Their flight touched down shortly after 1 PM, ensuring enough time to retrieve the rental car and check in at the same hotel. He was scheduled to arrive at 3 along with his special guest. They were getting more and more careless by booking trips together and out of office meetings at the same time. A blind man could put two and two together if needed.

Chateau Brevant was a luxurious boutique hotel located in the hills of Hollywood. Nightly rates for a hill view suite were $900 for 850 square feet. An intimate space with distinct personality greeted them. The padded leather headboard reached almost to the ceiling. A matching ottoman was nestled at the foot of the bed. Splashes of red paint with gold speckles emerged from either side of the headboard and overlaid the gold walls. One built in oval shaped ceiling light directly over the bed illuminated the room. It was as large as the bed. The bathroom matched the room in its exquisiteness. Marble covered every inch. The reflective gleam from the light added a touch of elegance. Multiple showerheads were mounted down the interior wall of glass-encased shower. It was a little bit of heaven on earth.

"Who in the hell stays in these kind of digs for a, quote-unquote, business meeting?" Gesturing with her hands, Gay fell back on the plush down comforter that immediately enveloped her small frame.

"You are right about that." Olivia concurred while diving on the bed beside her. "Nobody that we know personally. But I'm almost positive the few people that do either have money to blow or are trying to stay under the radar. Didn't you see all the twists and turns and hills and valleys we took just to get up here?"

"Yeah, a navigation system is a necessity for these parts."

Her personal phone rang before she could continue the conversation. Hold that thought. This is Rissa."

"What's up lady?

"Just making sure you two made it safely." Her well checks had become more frequent. "We are here at this expensive ass boutique. If it were up to us we'd be right at the Marriott but since it's not…" she chuckled.

"Olivia sent me a few pictures already. I think I'm going to look for something like that for our anniversary. Just out of the country."

"That would be really nice. Look at you trying to be all romantic and ish. I think that would be just what is needed. How is it going? Are things better?"

"He deserves it. Jonathan has been more than patient with me. Right now it's just a go with the flow kind of thing. I may be bailing on you before we even get started good. He's really not feeling this travel, night snooping or stake outs, as he calls it. He damn near flipped out when we were at training and I only texted instead of calling."

"I hate that for you. But I understand. This right here, which is not your bread and butter, can be walked away from at any time. You don't owe me a thing. I appreciate you stepping in and doing what you do."

Olivia, who was browsing social media, put her phone down to get a better ear of the conversation after she heard "walk away from". "Who? Rissa?" She asked Gay, whispering.

Gay raised her finger to indicate she would tell her in a minute once she got off the phone.

"It will work out."

"Hmmmm. You don't so sound too sure. Seriously, don't feel obligated to me. Your obligation is at home. That's your priority, but you already know that. Not sure why you haven't been acting like it, but if this scale is tipping over here, I need you to handle that."

"Are you using psychology on me?" A hint of Marissa's laughter could be heard in the room through the phone, like much of the conversation. "It sure does sound like it, and if you're not. I got it."

"Okay now. I don't have time for nobody breaking up. We still trying to get married over here, so hold on to the husband you have. All our husbands need to be boys like we are girls."

"That's lame, but it's still dope and would be so much fun."

"You think?"

"Yeah it would be fun. Bowling nights, cook outs,

getaways. All the fun stuff we used to do when we all were coupled up. You know, before some of us got all independent and self employed and didn't need no man anymore."

Olivia butted in. "Put her on speaker. Marissa, there she go. She tired of that chronically single status, so now she got so much to say about who should be doing what." They all erupted into laughter.

"I see it. Gay, it's always funny to hear you dish out relationship advice and ain't got a husband the first."

"See, you really didn't have to go there. Let's say I know what not to do if I don't want to be headed to divorce court a second time around. Just help me find another eye before you leave. And a boo for that matter."

"Ain't nobody said nothing about leaving, but I got you on that too. Church would be a good start."

"You are quite the fixer- upper. Oh and I got that church joke. You right, but I won't be going for no pimps in the pulpit. Let me try the club first."

"You told old for the club, boo. Let's try Starbucks then after you come to church with us."

"You are quite the jokester." The back and forth between the two was one of things that made their friendship so pure and organic. They could tell each other how they truly felt without the other getting upset. They could speak to each other in the safest of ways, free of judgment, without worries about broken English, Ebonics and all. Gay was concerned about her friend, although she wanted her to be there every step of the way with this missing child case. She also wanted her marriage to be solid and in tact. It was time for some babies.

When No One Came

A vibrating sound followed by two short rings could be heard from across the room. "Ok, gotta go! That's the office line. I could've sworn I rolled it over to Tressa."

"Bye Rissa." Olivia yelled at the phone before Gay hit end on the dial pad. A call to the office line meant new or old business. Gay jumped off the bed and grabbed her purse from the desk.

"GT Investigations. Gay Thibodeaux."

"Hi Gay. This is Jacqueline Mabrey. We spoke a few months ago about your agency assisting my family with finding our missing daughter. Are you able to come down?" Gay hadn't called as promised either way to inform her if she would take the case. There was progress but nothing significant. The Hawks needed to move.

"Good afternoon Mrs. Mabrey. Yes, we are planning to come to Florida for the community canvassing. Are there any new developments we need to be aware of?" Gay responded by answering the questions in way that allowed Olivia to know what was being asked before turning on the speakerphone.

"There is nothing new. We are still working to raise money for the reward fund and preparing for the community mobilization event. More people have been calling to say they want to help. We have a few radio and television interviews scheduled. Just need to get that done."

"How is that going? The fundraising" Gay didn't want that to sound like the focus but she knew money talked and as the old saying goes. Bullshit walks. Money had a way of attracting things. Just like when a person hits the lotto. Long lost cousins appeared. The long lost cousin or neighbor was desperately needed.

"Tony's job has committed 5 thousand. But we need more. I've seen rewards for missing children that are in the tens of thousands. Of course they aren't black."

"That's good to hear. I'm sure as work is done and more awareness is brought to the case more donations will come in. And, point taken on color."

"I'm praying. I really believe that more money will get people to talking because someone had to see or hear something."

"This could very well be true. We're going to work other angles in the meantime. You have to get people to love her like you do. Make them feel a sense of connection so they want to do more. Kinda like how you did at the meeting. From what you said happened and what is about to happen. There was a connection made. They had to see you all, parents feeling an unimaginable loss and a girl who deserves to be home with her parents."

"We've heard you are really good at what you do. We're counting on you to find our baby. We're counting on you to bring her home Ms. Thibodeaux." Mrs. Mabrey's voice cracked.

Silence fell over the room. Gay searched for the right response. By this time Olivia was sitting up in the bed staring in Gay's direction.

"I am good at finding people. This is new for me as I mentioned before. But I will try my best. We will try our best." Partially smiling at Marissa.

"We appreciate you for trying. We look forward to meeting you and your partners."

"We do as well. Please don't hesitate to call if anything

changes before we get there. Even if you think it's minor or not very significant. Let me be the judge."

"I will."

The two friends looked at each other for a minute before speaking. Tears rolled down Olivia's face. At that moment she got it. She thought about her client's that were children. Some of them she had been styling their hair since they were 4 and 5 years old. She thought about Gay's daughter who was close in age. Although she had no children of her own she couldn't imagine something happening to any one of them. She loved them like her own. There was something about the way Mrs. Mabrey said *I'm counting on you to bring her home* that touched her deeply. The plea from a mother grieving the loss of a child was overwhelming.

"Gay. I get it now. If I had a child and something happened to him or her I would want someone to help me as well. I would exhaust all options."

"I would too friend. I would too."

***

Sitting in the lobby waiting on Mr. CEO's arrival, the ladies sipped a glass of wine while strategizing their plans for Florida. With Marissa's issues on the home front and Tressa straddling the fence, Olivia was the only one left to go. She had called on a friend from Reno to see her clients for those few days. The friend had several stylists in her shop so it was easy for her to come over and just crash at Olivia's place. Olivia wouldn't make any money, but Gay agreed to pay her what she missed.

Looking down for a time check. Gay's watched read 4:15.pm. "They should be rolling in here any minute now. Like a doting couple I'm sure."

"You already know. When the mouse is away the cat will play. In this case the cat and the dog."

"Oh Olivia." Gay shook her finger. "Bad girl. But damn that was good."

They continued looking over maps and marked sections of the phone directory to personally call and addresses to visit. Monroe County wasn't that big and sounded like it was in the middle of nowhere. Definitely not close to any major cities that people were familiar with like Tampa, Orlando, or Miami. Their efforts would be grassroots beginning with a blank canvas. The first order of business was to meet with Detective Graham and the local sheriff, praying they would be met with very little resistance. Everybody was on the same team and it was up to them, The Hawks, to convince them.

A lady's laugh could be heard from across the room. Gay and Olivia looked up to see Mr. CEO and a very attractive woman walking towards the registration desk. Gay pulled out the camera pen and began taking pictures. The woman beside him was as tall as him, yet she wore 5-inch heels giving herself a few inches over him. Her mid length pencil skirt hugged her hips. The semi fitted blazer accented her small waist. A silver streaked bob haircut hung just below her ears. From a distance she was stunning and very well polished. All the photos on the web were on point. She looked the same. Careful research found that she was the mayor of Las Vegas, which explained the sporadic visits to Carson City. Las Vegas was over a 7-hour drive away.

The bellhop came to retrieve their bags. The ladies turned and began a pretentious conversation to avoid making eye and face contact with the two as they walked towards the bar. Noticeably a small black briefcase stayed with the two carried by Mr. CEO.

"You look flawless as always baby. Don't worry about going to the room and freshening up right now. Just be sure to wear that sexy black number to dinner tonight."

Poking him in the side she replied, "I gotcha number." She was obviously graying prematurely. Her body, face, and age told a different story. She barely pushed 50. Noted as the youngest and first African American woman to be elected the mayor of Las Vegas, this was her second term. From all news accounts and the department of revenue, she had brought in major money for the gaming and hotel industry. She worked hard to lobby to have some form of legal prostitution. There weren't too many complaints about it. Proponents argued that the place was called Sin City for a reason and it made no sense to try to start categorizing sin.

"And what's that?"

The playful exchange could be heard as they walked by. The woman up close was just as striking as from a distance. Her oversized shades hid her eyes, nonetheless, her cocoa colored skin was youthful and blemish free. A distinguished mole adorned the right side of her face just above the right lip, which were stained with a deep purple lippie. Mr. CEO was just as polished himself. The darkening of his goatee and hair added a bit of sex appeal. The weather was seasonably warm but it didn't deter him from being dressed in a dark blue suit with a paisley printed bowtie. The diamond cufflinks sparkled as the light hit them when he moved his arms. His dark brown shoes were polished. Free of scuffmarks and wear.

They were no longer within earshot. Watching from across the room Gay and Olivia both jotted down notes and recorded what they could without being too obvious. From time to time they would make a comment insuring that they were seeing and picking up on the same things. The glass of wine they had been nursing was now gone.

"We need to order another to keep these charades going." Gay shook her empty glass. "Let's give it a few, someone just may be joining them and I can walk to the bar then and maybe pick up on something."

They are quite the couple." Olivia couldn't help but comment. "I've never seen him interact with his wife like that."

"I've never seen him interact with his wife." The statement screamed sarcasm.

"Ouch Gay!"

"Well have you?" Gay brought her point home.

Shortly after Mr. CEO and his guest sat down and ordered drinks, two African American men joined them. The first man was dressed down in a Nike jumpsuit with matching shoes. He wore every piece of gold jewelry possible; watch, several necklaces, three rings on each hand, and hoop earrings. The meeting, from that moment on, smelled fishy. He was definitely an odd guest at the table. Flag on the field indeed.

"You wanna go?" Asking Olivia, Gay tilted her head towards the bar.

"You should. You would know better than me what to deduce from the conversation. What's happening now needs a more experienced eaves dropper."

"Since you put it that way." Slipping on her fake reading glasses and fixing her wig she proceeded to the bar area. Taking the long way around she wanted to be as near to the party as possible. Fortunately the bar area directly behind them was free of patrons.

The other man, appearing to be much older, was reserved in appearance. Salt and pepper colored locs hung past his shoulders. His face was clean-shaven. From the two Hawks vantage point from either side of the lobby he seemed to lead the conversation. Mr. CEO thumbed through a folder while the older gentleman spoke. At times the conversation became heated and teetered towards a full on shouting match. A gentle touch of the knee reined them back in with Mr. CEO lowering his voice. Pulling out a small envelope from his interior suit pocket, the older gentleman handed it to Mr. Cool who then passed it to Parker.

"Look through them. Tell me what's what by Friday. We need to make some moves. It's convention season." Gay made a mental note. Her hands were full with wine.

"Can I help you?" Mr. Cool stood up and walked towards her. "I'm fine. Thanks."

"Yeah I can see that," this time stepping in front of Gay's walking path.

"Thank you. Just headed back over to wait on my husband." She hoped that would get him off her. She continued to make mental notes.

The visit was brief with the two men leaving and taking the black briefcase with them.

MISSING PERSON #1

"We need you to count off by groups of 5. This is a delicate process." Detective Graham instructed the growing crowd. "Anyone who shows up after we begin searching this part of the woods will be given another task."

The community agreed to do bi-monthly active searches from the last meeting, pass out more flyers, and do door-to-door canvassing. Gay and Olivia flew down to Florida. They needed to be at ground zero to get a pulse on what occurred and to see what could be done to move the investigation forward. This seemed like a shot in the dark due to the length of time Josalyn had been missing, although there were rare occurrences of a missing child being found years later.

A makeshift command center was set up near the entrance. A pink tablecloth covered the table. Pink and Green balloons flew from either side. The pink symbolized Josalyn being a girl. The green balloons and ribbons on the table were a symbol to remember the missing child and to pray for a safe return. Wearing the ribbon also showed support and expressions of concerns for the family and other loved ones. The pink heart shaped donation jar was half full.

When No One Came

"Stay in a straight line, arm length from each other. Use the stick to probe areas that are covered with heavy brush, leaves, and other debris. We don't want to touch anything with our hands."

The crowd was full of nervous energy and mixed with those who hoped they could find something to help and others who feared finding something awful. A few seasons had passed since Josalyn's initial disappearance. The elements were sure to have washed away or broken down anything of significance.

"If you do come across something, even if you are unsure of what it is. Take the flag and mark it. The leader needs to call or blow the whistle and we will come. Any questions?

The only thing that could be heard was shifting of the feet, cars passing by, dogs barking in the distance and environmental sounds like the wind blowing and leaves rustling.

"Ok, let's go! It's 1:00 now." Detective Graham looked at his watch and set the timer. "Walk as far as you can for two hours. Then turn and come back following the same guidelines. Be sure to take plenty of water."

The crowd moved in silence. Having decided not to participate in the search, the Hawks visited the Mabreys instead, but not before introducing themselves to Detective Graham who appeared more than eager to meet with them.

"Detective Graham," extending her hand. "I'm Gay Thibodeaux and this is one of my business partners, Olivia Marston. We are from GT Investigations in Carson City, Nevada."

"Yes, I've been expecting you." His handshake was firm. The older white man spoke with confidence and if Gay didn't know any better his chest was a little pumped up. It was known that top officials in law enforcement were territorial and didn't take to kindly to someone else in the field sticking their noses in their business. It insinuated incompetence even more so to those who really were slacking on the job. "You ladies are a long way from home and you definitely don't fit the bill of being a private investigator. Too pretty for that."

"Stereotyping are we?"

"No ma'am. Just calling it how I see it. But that's not a bad thing is it?"

"Only if you think pretty faces are all we have to offer." Olivia tried not to show that she was offended.

"Ok, let's start over. No harm, no foul." Detective Graham offered an olive branch. "It's a pleasure to meet you both. What interests you about this case? What brings you here?"

Gay paused ensuring her response would not offend him while fostering the idea of camaraderie. The goal was to find Josalyn and bring her home safely. All stops had to be pulled. "There isn't one single thing about this case that interests us. First and foremost we are here at the request of the family. I'm sure you are aware that is hardly unusual for families to request independent investigations when a crime has been committed. So it's definitely not to slight you or your office."

"Yes, I understand. I just wish they had spoken to me. I'm not sure you all can or will find something that we haven't already."

"That is yet to be seen." Gay responded. "Let's not rush to judgment."

"No offense."

"None taken."

Gay offered insight to Detective Graham's uneasiness about the family having not consulted with him prior to contacting the Hawks. "I do believe that the family just wants to get as many eyes on this case as possible without jeopardizing the integrity of it. I gathered that the communication between you all has been a bit relaxed."

"What do you mean?"

"There seems to be more asking than telling. More initiative on their part to stay on top of the case."

"That's a fair assessment. We are just working on so many cases and items of business from petty theft, to serving warrants, to recruitment. But it's still no excuse. In my 16 years of being in law enforcement and in my 35 years of living here this is the first missing child case I've heard of and worked. It's baffling to have a child disappear out of thin air."

"Will you let us help?" Gay asked almost pleading.

"It can't hurt." Detective Graham conceded. "We should finish here about 4:30 this afternoon. Come by the station then. I will call to have all the case notes put in the conference room for you. I can't let you take anything or photo copy what we have but you are free to take your own notes."

"That will do."

"Call me on my cell if you need anything before I get there. Have you met the Mabreys yet?"

"We are on our way there now."

***

"Why were you giving that man the evil eye?" Gay laughed.

"Was I?"

"Evil eye times 10."

"I was just a little offended that he didn't take us seriously. That seems to be a reoccurring theme these days. It's not 1960. Women are holding down some of the same jobs as men. Hell we running the company these days."

"I agree. Just don't let it get under your skin. We do have to work extra hard in proving ourselves but until we show them we can't, let them keep thinking that and bring the thunder. We're here. Right?"

"You're right."

"You need a hug?"

"Not right now but I suspect before this day is over I will."

"Got it on reserve."

"Thanks Gay."

"For."

"Being you. Being a voice of reason. For showing up."

"Don't go getting all mushy on me."

The Rockport community was huge. It consisted of several small subdivisions within the subdivision. Some of the entrances were gated and from the road sprawling 4 side brick homes could be seen. The lawns were well manicured; mulch and pine straw covered the bases of trees and bushes. Some lawns had rocks and bricks outlining the shrubbery. Landscape lighting enhanced the yards as they lined the driveways and walkways. Many of the homes had decks with top of the line patio furniture others had rocking chairs on the porch and doors embellished with monogram wreaths. Women jogged along pushing strollers, and children rode bikes with their parents walking alongside them.

"What's the address again? Gay stopped to turn on the GPS.

"3242 Millcreek Dr."

Before inputting the address Gay looked up and across the street to see pink and green balloons flying from a mailbox. "I think we have found our home."

"I think we have."

The Mabreys didn't live behind the gate. Their two-story home had a brick face and hardy plank siding. The yard was well groomed as the others. Pulling into the drive the ladies both took two deep breaths.

"Let me say a quick prayer." Olivia didn't wait for Gay to reply and grabbed her hand. "Father God we thank you again for safe travels. I thank you for Gay and her willingness to try new things. For her being a truth seeker. We thank you for discernment. We thank you for supernatural ears and eyes to be able to hear the gentle whispers and to see those things that only you can reveal to us. Let us not get overwhelmed with emotion and wrapped up in self. You brought us here to do you work. We pray that resolve comes soon for this family and that whatever your will is that they are okay. Prepare us for the same will as well. Give us the right words of comfort. Let this meeting be fruitful and that we all go to the next place renewed and empowered for the task at hand, however hopeless it may seem. In your son Jesus' name, I, Olivia Marston ask of you. Amen."

Gay, a person who rarely cried could not hold back the tears. She was now at the moment and place she had worried over for the past few months. It was surreal. "Amen. I think I can use a hug now."

Olivia unbuckled her seat beat and leaned over to oblige. "It's go time. Take a moment and let me know when you are ready."

Pressing down on the inside corners of her eyes with the Kleenex to dry up the tears and prevent anymore from falling Gay breathed out and then in. "It's go time."

A few children's toys were on the porch. It was obvious they belonged to Josalyn and had been there for some time. Everything else was in place. The front door had a large oval window in the middle. The curtain was pulled back which allowed any visitor to see throughout the house. A medium framed woman with her hair in a bun opened the door before Gay could ring the doorbell.

"Hi. How can I help you?"

"Mrs. Mabrey?"

"Yes."

"I'm Gay Thibodeaux and this is Olivia."

"We've been waiting on you. I've run to the door every time I heard a car pass by or get near the house. Tony said I was making him nervous and he's usually the calm one. Come on in." She stepped aside and opened the door wider. The smell of a home cooked meal greeted them. "Tony! The ladies are here. Tony!"

Tony appeared in the hall. "Yes dear. I heard. It's a pleasure meeting you?" He extended his hand unsure of who was who.

"Gay Thibodeaux."

"Olivia Marston."

They both extended their hand before being led to the great room. "Please have a seat. Can I get you anything to drink? Are you hungry?" Mrs. Mabrey offered.

"Jackie I will take care of it. Have seat. You've been up for a while now." Tony insisted.

"Water is fine." Gay looked towards Olivia who nodded as well.

"We have tea and lemonade as well."

"Thank you. Water is fine."

"Anything to eat? Jackie has been cooking since early this morning. With the canvassing going on she wasn't sure if people would be stopping by. It gave her something to do also."

"We might grab a plate to go. We are due at the station in a few hours." The ladies hadn't eaten since they touched down, but nerves seemed to have gotten the best of them. Their appetites were gone. "Whatever you cooked does smell delicious." Olivia smiled as she continued the small talk to ease the tension.

"How was the flight?" Mrs. Mabrey asked.

"No crying babies, no rough turbulence, no snoring aisle buddy. I would say it was great. Wouldn't you agree Gay?" Olivia laughed at herself and the two other ladies quickly joined in.

"I agree silly."

Steering the conversation back to business Gay directed her next question to Mrs. Mabrey. "Mrs. Mabrey thank you again for reaching out. We are truly humbled. We want to go into this with all cards on the table. What exactly do you expect from us?" Gay put it out there. The last thing they wanted was an assumption or expectation of something that could not be delivered.

Tony stood in the doorway. "Come on in honey." Mrs. Mabrey motioned for him to sit beside her. "That's a tough question but it's a fair question. In a perfect world or a make believe world we expect you to find our daughter and bring her home. Untouched, undefiled, and looking exactly how she did the last time we saw her."

"We appreciate your honesty." It was easier to respond for both as they were on the same page. "But let's speak from the now world. From where we are with what we have." Gay prodded for a more concrete, tangible response."

This time Mr. Mabrey spoke. "Yes we understand that it may be far fetched. But we believe in a God that has been in the miracle working business for a long time. We don't question why this has happened. You know we both work hard, we treat people the right way, and we love our neighbors. Those simple things can carry a person far and we have worked hard to teach Josalyn the same things. So what do we expect from you?" He paused and bit his lip. It was clear he was a God fearing man and he loved and his missed his daughter as much as his wife. After all, daddies were protectors.

"Ladies, we don't intend to put any undue pressure on you. Yes we want our daughter home, safely. But we also know that you all can only do what is humanely possible. We just ask that you all do your best, you fight for Josalyn as if she were your child, don't take no for answer, don't leave a stone unturned, and

When No One Came

tell us the truth, even if it will hurt us." Mrs. Mabrey pleaded through the tears.

Mr. Mabrey rubbed his wife's back through his own tears. "Whatever it costs. Just do your best."

Gay and Olivia fought to hold back their own tears. Their heart ached for them. Looking at pictures of Josalyn reminded her of her sweet 10-year-old Naja. They both had teeth that were still settling in. They were in that growth phase were the teeth looked bucked and too big for their mouths. They both had shoulder length hair that was usually styled in 1 or 2 ponytails, similar brown skin and smiles. Yes Gay ached and her head hurt.

"We can look at cost later. Your candor is appreciated. Trust and know we will do our best." Olivia and Gay had both walked over to them and kneeled in front of them. Olivia held Mrs. Mabrey's and Gay Mr. Mabrey's.

No one spoke for a while. "We need to get as much as information as possible before we head to the station. It's been a while but whatever details you can provide about that day would help tremendously."

Olivia placed a tape recorder on the coffee table. Gay grabbed a notebook and the camera. "Do you mind if I look around in Josalyn's room for a bit?"

"No problem. It's the second room on the left immediately off the stairs." Mr. Mabrey pointed in that direction.

"Mrs. Mabrey let's begin with you. Tell me everything you remember about that day. No detail is too small. We need to know what you were doing. What times? What was the weather like? Do you recall any neighbors being outside? Did anyone call you?" Olivia pressed record.

Josalyn's room was pink, yellow, and purple. The butterfly theme was whimsical. The entire room from the bedding to the furniture had butterfly accents. The hand-painted butterflies on the wall were very detailed. The veins on the wings made them appear life like. Gay stood in the middle of the room and looked around. Shoes were on the floor and uniform on the bed. This was typical after school behavior when children came home and swapped their school clothes for their play clothes. The room was undisturbed. While taking pictures of the room and everything it contained, the aching began to revisit Gay's heart.

Clutching her chest, Gay sat on the floor beside the shoes. One of the black leather shoes was upright and the other was lying on its side. The inside label read Hush Puppy size 4. Gay picked up the small shoe and held it in her hands. The scuffed toes showed that Josalyn was an active 10 year old. A survey of the room, the closet, and drawers and underneath the bed revealed nothing more than she was a typical girl full of innocence. Dolls, books, markers, journals, stuffed animals, and a tablet with heart stickers covering the outside confirmed and gave no further insight on who could have taken her. Before leaving Gay took a picture off the desk and slid in her notebook.

Mrs. Mabrey's voice carried to the top of the stairs. Looking down Gay could see Mr. Mabrey standing at an angle where he could see up the stairs and into the great room. "Did anything jump out at you?" He didn't hesitate to ask.

"Nothing. Your baby is just a precious little girl that likes pretty things." Gay referred to Josalyn in the present tense.

Mr. Mabrey mustered a smile across his tired face. Family pictures from a year ago and his face at present showed a man who had aged in a relatively short time. There was more gray, wrinkles, and dark circles under his eyes. He continued to work

When No One Came

while coming home to be there emotionally and mentally for Mrs. Mabrey who had taken an extended leave of absence. "We thank you. I don't think we can say it enough."

"You don't have to. We are here because we want to be." The two briefly embraced one another. "Olivia, I'm finished upstairs. If you're done I think it's time we head over to the station."

"We just finished up."

"Here are the pictures you asked for." Handing the pictures to Olivia Mr. Mabrey lowered his head.

"Ladies we won't hold you. We know you have lots of work to do. We will be right here if you have more questions or need anything."

Olivia looked down the street and at the neighboring homes before she got in the car. A woman a few houses down stood in the yard waving her hand. "Mrs. Mabrey, Olivia called from the driveway. Do you know who's waving? Is she trying to get your attention?"

"That's Widow Jones. She's what we call the neighborhood watch. She feigns old and senile but I believe she has more sense than the young folk."

"Is that right?" Olivia's interest peaked. Just like in the movies the older folk usually see and hear it all but are overlooked because of their age. "Do you know if anyone spoke to her?"

"Detective Graham said he did but didn't get much. I didn't see her out that day so it didn't dawn on me to ask her anything."

"We'll stop. It looks like she has something to say and will give you a call sooner rather than later."

Olivia drove this time, easing the rental car into the driveway. Both ladies got out and greeted the widow.

"Were you trying to get our attention?"

"Sure I was?" The frail woman nodded her head. She was unable to stand up tall and straight but her eyes were bright and her smile showed a nice set of dentures. Standing in her duster and house shoes on the lawn she went on to say. "You girls aren't from around here."

"No ma'am. How did you know?"

"I see the same cars everyday all the time. I see the same folk too and you girls ain't the same folk."

"Well you are right about that." Gay engaged her. "You were waving to us. Did you just want to speak?"

"Who just wants to speak to strangers child? I may be old but I ain't crazy. Folk will hurt you these days with no remorse and I don't trust these police. They won't do a damn thang to help you." Widow Jones snarled.

"Okay. How can we help?"

"You tell me. You over there trying to help Tony and Jackie ain't ya?"

"Yes."

"Well what do you want to know?"

Gay's patience was wearing thin. "Please tell us what you think we should know. Did you see anything they day Josalyn went missing?"

"I sure did." Olivia ran to the car to grab the recorder.

"Can you speak into this?" Holding the recorder close to Widow Jones' face.

"Wait a minute now. I don't want to have to go to no court and do all that testifying."

"You won't have to." Gay wasn't sure if that would be the case but for now she needed to know whatever Widow Jones knew.

"Well two boys or maybe men. They didn't look too old. Kept riding through here. They were in a white van that said something about painting. Maybe they was working on somebody house. Or maybe they was looking for work. I don't know but the van came by here for two days and after that I didn't see it anymore."

"Have you told anybody else this?"

"I mentioned it to that white boy. Detective Graham I think that's his name. He kept asking all about license plates and stuff. Do I look like I just stand out here with a pen and paper writing down that kinda stuff?"

"No ma'am. Anything else you can remember about that day?"

"That's it and I told them about it. Are y'all gonna help Jackie and Tony?"

"We're going to try."

"I hope so. They are so sad. Jackie don't even come out the house. She useta would brang me cakes and pies and thangs and send that sweet girl down here."

"Yes ma'am. Here is my card if you remember anything else. I circled the number for you and wrote it again on the back. You should go and sit with Mrs. Mabrey for a spell. I'm sure she would appreciate your company."

"I just might."

***

Police cars, a newspaper reporter, and a crime scene investigation van were parked near the entrance of the woods. A crowd of people stood around talking amongst themselves. Gay recognized some of the faces from earlier. The increased activity could have only meant that something had been found.

"Detective Graham?"

"Yes."

"This is Gay. We were leaving and noticed an up tick in activity near the woods. What's going on?"

"If you are still in the neighborhood stop by and I will come up to meet you."

"We are pulling over now and will be beside the CSI van."

"On my way."

Gay and Olivia sat anxiously waiting, each running through their own minds thoughts about what had been found and silently praying that it was nothing too devastating. They were so lost in these thoughts they did not see Detective Graham approach the car.

Startled by the tap on the driver's side window they both jumped. Their nerves were rattled and the work was just beginning.

Detective Graham stepped aside to allow enough room for Olivia to get out of the car. He could see the questions in their eyes and the uneasiness on their faces. "We found two bikes. I've sent someone down to the Mabrey's to get a picture of the bike or to come and let us know if one of them belonged to Josalyn."

"Have you all searched this area before?" Gay asked.

"We've done a scan but the more intensive searches have taken place closer to the wooded area in the rear of the community. Near the Mabrey home."

Gay secretly hoped that the Mabreys would send a picture to identify the bike. Already on a brink of breakdown seeing their child's bike in the woods was sure to put them over the top.

"Let's head down."

"Olivia will you grab the camera pen?" Gay whispered in her ear having remembered the earlier conversation of no photo copying the evidence she was sure taking pictures of a potential crime scene or evidence was a no go.

"We're right behind you."

The wooded area being searched was not too far from a paved walking trail. The ground was covered with leaves from the spring. Summer had not gotten into full swing yet so it was still a little damp. Piles of wet leaves were dispersed throughout and off the path, the area was hilly with a few drop off areas.

"One of the bikes is over there. Just behind that tree, the tallest one in the middle. The other is a little farther down on the left." Detective Graham pointed to the right. "Be careful the depth is deceiving with all the leaves and brush."

The area was taped off with yellow crime scène tape. A tarp covered the ground while someone that worked in law enforcement took pictures before the bike and some leaves were moved over to it for more photographing. Two men hoisted a pink bike from the ravine. The tires were deflated and the rear wheel was bent. Dirt and rust covered it. The leather seat was cracked and dry. One handlebar was missing streamers. A few hung on the other. The plastic was obviously not biodegradable. The brand could not be made out but there was a small decorative rusted metal tag similar to license plate attached to the front. The color was worn off but the indentions or marking from the stamp was still visible.

"I'm okay. Just let me see the bike. Let me see if it's Josalyn's." Mr. Mabrey had made it to the woods.

At the same time the investigators were bringing the other bike up on a tarp as well. "We need everyone to clear this area out with the exception of those actively working this discovery. I also need someone to go up and do crowd control. Thank the people and send them home." Detective Graham expressed his frustration. "Let Tony by."

"This one is hers." Standing over the bikes. He pointed at the one that was further down. It was in better condition due to having been covered with black plastic bags. It didn't have a tag or anything but there was a light on the back that Tony had added when he bought it. There was no visible sign of blood or anything on either bike. "That's my baby girl's bike. Did you all find anything else?"

"Nothing else. But now we know that she was in this area with someone. We just need to ask more questions and work this area. Someone has seen something."

"Mr. Mabrey. We will stay another day and talk to the

people who live nearby." Olivia reassured. "I'm sure it's not what you wanted to hear or see but it could be much worse. It could be final."

UNWELCOME VISITOR

The cigar hung loosely from his mouth as he scrolled through his phone leaning against the building with one foot propped up behind him. A baseball cap hung low over his eyes. He took the cigar out of his mouth and went straight into a coughing fit followed by blowing his nose profusely. The smoke seemed to be giving his lungs all kinds of fits. Taking one draw he finally snuffed it out on the ground before entering the restaurant. This vice was obviously costing him his health. Stooping to avoid hitting his head, he continued to cough as he passed over the threshold. The strange man looked out of place as with most tourists. His dressed was more indicative of South Beach- Bermuda shorts, flip flops and a button down shirt.

Making his way to the bar he looked around slowly. Almost like he was looking for a familiar face or was planning to meet someone. "Got a light?" Bypassing the formal greeting.

"Sorry buddy Carson City is a smoke free zone."

"And?"

"That means you can't light up inside bars and restaurants.

When No One Came

Some restaurants have taken it a step further where you can't light up within 10 feet of the main entrance."

"You don't say?"

"Yep, it's a new health officer in town. Working on his legacy I suppose."

"That's really got to hurt the bars revenue. You know people go to bars for a stiff drink, a smoke or two, catch a date, and maybe a game on the big screen."

"That sounds about right. I got all of the above except the smoke. What'll you have?"

"Let me get a rum and coke on the rocks with a splash of lemon."

"Coming right up. Do you want to order something to eat?"

"Uh, not right now."

The peculiar stranger looked through his phone before placing a call. "Hey, I'm at the spot. You say they usually come in around this time. But this place is dead as a doorknob. Nothing's shaking." He nodded as he listened to the person on the other end.

"Yeah, I know. I'll give it a few more minutes before I head back to the hotel."

"Excuse me." Calling the bartender over. "Do you know a woman by the name of Gay? She's a regular here."

"Who wants to know?"

"Oh we went to high school together. Yeah back in New York. I heard she lived out here now. Since I was passing through I thought I'd look her up. You know, say hi and all."

"Oh, I see. Nah, that name doesn't ring a bell. Rum and coke on the rocks with a splash of lemon. That'll be $9."

Something didn't sit right with Jason about the stranger. Not only was his questioning odd it just didn't seem like he was the kind of friend she would have in high school. He looked to have graduated long before she did. The hair on his head and beard were almost snow white. The crow's feet around his eyes were deep and long. Years of smoking had stained his teeth yellow. He was old and up to no good.

"Keep the change." The stranger handed him a $20."

"Thanks, I didn't get your name."

"Bob, yeah just Bob."

"Thanks again Bob. I gotta few glasses to wash. I'll be at the end of the bar if you need me."

Bob nodded his head and took a sip of his drink. "Nice."

Jason, growing suspicious of Bob, whipped out his phone and pretended to be placing a call to his girlfriend.

"Hey Jay. What's up?" He and Gay, along with the other ladies, had been friends since they moved there. Almost like family. He attended birthday parties, weddings, outings, and more. From time to time they would drive over to Vegas for the weekend just for the fun of it. Occasionally he would be her eyes and ears.

"Hey babes. How's your day going?'

"Jason I think you dialed me by accident this is Gay."

"Yep, that's good to hear. Did you ever find the info about

When No One Came

the class reunion?"

"Class reunion? Heeellllo, this is Gay."

"Yep, I think you should go. I'm sure your classmates would love to see you. I'm ready to meet a few myself. It's crazy knowing someone else's life story while never having met them."

"Ok- you're freaking me out now. What's going on?"

"Yeah, just thought about it. A guy is here now having a drink and looking for one of his high school classmates. Passing through he says."

"Is someone there looking for me?" Gay finally caught on.

"How'd you know?"

"What does he look like?"

"Trouble. Yeah I think that can get you in a world of trouble if you do that." The riddles continued.

"Take a picture on the sly and call me when he leaves. See if you can see what kind of car he's driving too."

"Never mind me. I'm just a jealous boyfriend."

"Don't let him see you."

"Love you more."

The stranger beckoned for Jason. "Tell Gay I stopped by and don't worry her pretty little head. I'll be back. Here's my card." Dropping the card on the bar's counter top he stood and gulped that last corner of his drink, pulled at the bib of the baseball cap as to bid a farewell and turned to leave before Jason could ask a question or further deny knowing Gay.

The door flew open before he could push outward causing him to lose his balance. Hitting his head on the frame he fell onto Marissa. She and Tressa both broke his fall.

"Sorry about that. We were just running our mouths and not paying attention at all."

"No problem ladies." Rubbing the top of his head a closer look revealed this was half of the quad he was looking for. "Why don't I let you two buy me a drink? For the pain and suffering?" He winked.

"Too funny." They didn't recognize him. "I don't remember seeing you before. Are you a newbie?" Marissa probed.

"You can say that. How about that drink now." Bob insisted.

"We don't parlay with folk we don't know. But if you really want a drink. We can put $20 down to start you a tab at the bar. We're actually waiting on a few friends so we won't be able to join you."

"Let's break it up over there. You all coming in or going out." Jason yelled over the bar to them. He was sure not to call them by name and hoped they picked up on the fact that something was wrong. Per usual especially when it was slow, he would have fixed their drinks and walked them over to their regular table. This time he stayed behind the bar.

"Well the man has spoken. What say you beautiful ladies?"

"Excuse me, we didn't get your name." Tressa asked with a curious look on face. Although the question was directed at Bob she looked at Marissa when she asked. Intuition was setting in.

When No One Came

Jason remaining behind the bar kicked it up a notch. They didn't call his name either pretending they didn't know him.

Still holding the door open and carrying on the conversation the tall rough appearing man stepped back. "My name is Bob. And you ladies are?"

"We would have never guessed. You don't look like a Bob." Marissa was calling his bluff. The set was all wrong. "Like we said before, we're waiting on friends but will be more than happy to get you a drink on our dime. You just have to drink alone."

"Somebody listened to momma and daddy I see. Stranger danger."

"Excuse us." Marissa stepped around pulling Tressa with her leaving Bob holding the door.

"Thanks for the hospitality." He pulled at the cap's bib again. "Stranger danger."

MISSING PERSON #2

Phones ringing, officers sitting at desks, a few blue uniforms escorted handcuffed alleged law breakers to the booking area or holding cells, inaudible voices broke through the scanner. The police station, however small, was quite busy and noisy for a Thursday afternoon. The main desk was nestled about 10 feet from the main entrance.

An almost unrecognizable Doris Langston walked in. The brown overcoat that fit snugly the previous fall now hung on her loosely. Her dark and sunken eyes told the story of a hurting and grieving mother that hadn't slept in quite some time. She had gone back to work on limited duty having been reassigned to mostly deskwork.

"Good afternoon Ms. Langston." The front desk officer greeted her. In previous months, she had become almost a fixture at the station, being sure to stop by before work, after work and on lunch breaks. After being forced back to work having exhausted all her accrued personal leave and the leave donated by her colleagues, her drop-ins were less frequent.

Through clenched teeth Doris asked, "Any updates?" While

When No One Came

looking at Dynasty's missing poster that still hung on the corkboard in the main lobby. The lone page had begun to yellow from the sunlight, Much like something that had been left unattended over time. "Any updates?" She asked again this time leaning on the counter.

The officer's eyes followed hers as she stared at the poster again before turning back to the desk. "No ma'am. We thought we had a lead but it turned out to be a case of mistaken identity. I promise you we are doing all we can." The responses began to sound like a broken record.

"When did that happen? Why didn't you call me?"

"It was one day last week. We wouldn't call on that. It would have to be a little more concrete. Otherwise we would be calling all the time."

"And I'm okay with that."

"I don't think you would be okay with false hope and possibilities. Of being let down every day because we thought we had something. That kind of emotional roller coaster just isn't good for anyone."

"You should let me decide." Ms. Langston spoke in aggravated tone.

"Yes ma'am. We are doing all we can."

She spoke hollow words hidden behind dark, pit like eyes. "I don't think you are. It's been over six months. The seasons have changed. Folks have moved into town and out of town. And the response is always the same. If I'm not asking the questions nobody is. Did you all speak to everyone at the dance that night? What about the group of kids driving around the parking lot that didn't even attend the school? Did you even know that happened?"

"The lead detective has worked every angle." Searching for the right tone to offer reassurance, the officer really didn't know for sure if he had done everything Ms. Langston asked about, but played it safe by sticking with the standard response. For a rural town with a population of under a thousand that was code for we do what we can, with what we have, when we can.

"We had the talk. She had my lines memorized. No you can't catch a ride with so and so even if their momma says it's ok. I promised not to have her waiting long." Tears fell. "That damn train..." Doris turned to leave before completing the sentence. Her walk was slow, yet steady.

The officer called to her. "Ms. Langston. I know you have probably been asked this before. I'm asking to try to make sense of this myself. Did you and Dynasty have a fight or something? Could she have left on her own? You know how these girls get when they hit puberty?"

"These girls? These girls that you speak of are not my Dynasty. Being a woman who works in the community, what are you doing to help these girls you speak of? I don't ever recall seeing you patrol the neighborhood, yet you make a blanket insulting comment like that." Ms. Langston seethed at the very thought.

"I'm sorry if I implied that your daughter was like the rest."

"I don't think you are. It's always an assumption that if a black girl comes up missing it's because something is going on in the home, especially if it's a single parent home."

"I'm not saying that. I just know that this town isn't but yea big. Stuff like this seems to happen only in the big cities."

"Child why are you here? You don't seem to have your pulse on what is going on in this world; big city, little city, white, black or yellow. Crime doesn't care about none of it. And while you are gathering your facts be sure to read the file on Dynasty Langston, the athlete, the honor roll student, the dancer, the gymnast, choir member- church and school, the student council president, Beta club." Tallying all that Dynasty was involved with on her fingers she asked, "Do I need to go on?"

"No ma'am." Her voice lowered with embarrassment.

"Does that sound like a girl who would just pack up and leave? Does it even sound like a girl who would even fight with her momma?

"No ma'am."

"Are you saying that a runaway is no more important than a child who was kidnapped? Help me understand the rationale behind the question and why that was even a thought." Ms. Langston was relentless.

"Please don't be offended." The officer asserted. She had opened a can of worms she had not intended to open, and Ms. Langston was not interested in sparing feelings. She had been patient and accommodating for too long. "My reason for asking was out of genuine concern. A runaway is still a missing child that could be in danger, so no, I wasn't implying that one life was valued over the other. I do know that if the child is a runaway they aren't usually too far. There have been cases that a child was found at a friend's home. Just maybe some friends haven't been questioned because they only looked at it from a kidnapping angle. I'm making assumptions."

"Well I appreciate your concern, but it seems you have some more training to do. That's why you," pointing at the officer, "sit at this desk, I assume." Ms. Langston then tapped the desk with that same finger." She was livid.

"I'll accept that."

"And while you are accepting, stop assuming. You don't get paid to assume. Assuming doesn't help me find my daughter one single bit. Now, if you would, let Chief Buckner know I came by and I *will* be back tomorrow."

Leaving feeling even more defeated than when she came, Mrs. Langston looked up to see Chief Buckner pull into his reserved parking space. She waited outside, near the entrance. Before he could get one leg out of the car, she called out, " Chief Buckner," ensuring he saw her and that he knew she was waiting on him. "Chief Buckner." She called and waved again.

"Hello Ms. Langston. I'm glad that I didn't miss you this time."

She was over the small talk. "So am I. Why aren't there any updates? I keep getting the same thing while this case is getting colder and colder like the weather. She's been missing since June and now it's October."

"I understand your frustration."

"Save it. I'm so sick of tired of people telling me that understand when we know good and well you and the rest of them don't understand a darned thing. To understand would mean you have had a child stolen from you. To understand just may mean that you have lost a child. Well have you."

"No I haven't but that doesn't mean I don't have empathy for you and what you're going through."

"Save the empathy and do something. I'm sorry but I don't

care about your empathy." Her enough had arrived.

"Actually there is something. Let's go into my office."

Those words were bitter sweet. Ms. Langston had longed to hear there were new developments while at the same time dreading them.

"I'm not sure if you aware but there were a group of kids riding around the schools parking lot after the dance. These kids didn't attend the high school and weren't from the area. We have reason to believe Dynasty got in the car with them, possibly not on her own."

"What does that mean?"

"A number of students reported becoming ill after drinking punch. Groggy, sleepy, slurred speech. Some parents believed that their children had been given alcohol at the dance. We later found out it wasn't alcohol but Spanish fly or a similar derivative."

"Spanish fly? Folk were using that back in the 70's. How did these kids get their hands on that? And are you saying Dynasty was given that?"

"I'm not saying that. What I am saying is that we are following up to see if her behavior was strange and if she got in the car with those boys? We don't even know who they are."

"Why has it taken so long?"

"Ms. Langston, you have to understand, the last thing many of the kids will do is let their parents know they were doing something they had no business doing- and if that means lying and hiding something, then so be it."

"Even when a life is at stake?"

"Even if a life is at stake, sadly." Chief Buckner answered. "We will be at the school tomorrow going through the list of everyone who bought a ticket again. Now that we know what we do, hopefully they will come clean and tell us everything we need to know to get Dynasty back home where she belongs."

"What can I do? I know many of the parents."

"We don't need you to do anything but trust the process. It's long and hard but we have to do it right. I will be in touch. Go home and get some rest, please Doris."

***

"Ms. Langston." An unfamiliar voice called from the distance. "Ms. Langston."

She turned to see an African American man in his mid thirties walking towards her. "My name is Clyde Owens. I've been following your story. I work for the South Carolina Free Press. I would like to interview you and run your story again if possible."

"I will take you up off on your offer." Her voice didn't change in tone.

"Also I have some information that may be useful for you." Reaching into wallet he retrieved a card and handed to her. "The lady that owns this firm is a private investigator. She's located in Nevada but from what I hear she's one of the best."

"She sounds expensive."

"I'm not sure, but it wouldn't hurt to give her a call. She may be able to get this case warm again. From what I gather, and by the look on your face after leaving the station, you could use that kind of person."

"You're right and I appreciate your concern or are you chasing a story."

"Well I am doing my job, but I'm also concerned about Dynasty and I want to see a happy ending. I would like to report a happy ending for a change. Here is my card. Let's get the story back in the headlines. I can also call my colleague at the news station in Charlotte to see if we can get you some airtime."

"Thank you." Unable to muster much more, Ms. Langston shook his hand, took his card, and walked towards her car.

MISSING PERSON #3

"Davion Brooks. Look at the picture. Remember his face. He's my son and I want him home. I need him home."

News vans and trucks lined the streets of 7 Mile and Grand for a second day. Reporters and cameramen stood on the lawn of 825 Grand waiting for someone to appear from the small all brick colonial style home.

"Davion Brooks." Ronnie Brooks held an 8.5 by 11 sheet of paper in front of the camera while calling his son's name. "Where have you been Channel 2? Channel 5? Mike Robinson?"

"Mr. Brooks? Mr. Brooks is there anything you would like for the viewers at home to know about your son?"

"Where have you been? I've been calling for a days now and all I get is, "we will run the story." I watch the news everyday at 6 in the morning, 12 noon and 6 in the evening. Nothing."

"We are here now. What would you like the viewers to

know?"

"I would like then to know that my 14 year old son is like any other kid. He can be a knucklehead sometimes, no he's not an honor roll student, I have to get on him about his chores, and who he hangs with, but, you know, he's no gang banger, no trouble maker."

With the camera panning back and forth between the two the reporter looked startled. "Ok. Thank you for that."

"What did you expect me to say? My kid's human. He's a typical teen. I'm not going to get out here and paint the picture like he's perfect. All that doesn't matter. He's my son. I work hard to provide for him and keep him on the right path. And whoever has him or knows where he is, let him go, send him home. And Davion if you can hear my voice. I'm not mad at you. Just come on home."

"So are you saying you all had a disagreement and he left?"

"I'm not saying that. And what does that matter? He's been gone for two days and ain't nobody rallying trying to get him home."

"Where's his mother?"

"I knew this would happen. Y'all reporters like to focus on all the negative. Everything you asking me has absolutely nothing to do with the fact that my 14-year-old son hasn't been home or called home in two days. Can you show his picture again? Tell the people where he was last seen? Tell them what he was last seen wearing? Then get the hell off my yard!"

Mr. Brooks turned to walk in the house disgusted at how the media had just turned the disappearance of his son into a three-ring circus. It was true he had made some disparaging remarks about the lack of coverage and support he was receiving. Sadly enough, his own family didn't take it seriously. Apparently children left home for two and three days at time in Detroit. The cause for worry didn't happen until the days turned into weeks. Things had changed since Ronnie had last lived there some twenty odd years ago. A growing recession was taking a toll on the metropolitan area. While Ford, GM and Chrysler remained the top three employers, residents were leaving in droves. There was a mass exodus.

This was better than the alternative for Ronnie and Davion. Davion was being swallowed up in the gang violence and crime in Chicago. Fearing that Davion wouldn't live to see his 18th birthday had they stayed, Ronnie packed up to be near family that could lend a hand in raising him. After making it to Detroit he soon realized he had jumped out of the frying pan into the fire, now amidst a different kind of violence and poverty.

A small crowd gathered on the sidewalk, watching-- as if the plea for a missing child was a spectator sport of sorts. "Ronnie." Someone called from the crowd. "We gotcha back. What you wanna do?"

Turning to see who it was, Ronnie nodded at his first cousin and motioned for him to come inside with him. "Where you been?"

"I just made it back. The car broke down and was dealing with that. Did you hear Dawn's son is missing too?"

"Yeah they were together."

"Word?" Why ain't nobody talking about that? Two boys missing instead of one might get more attention especially since they was last seen together."

"You know I can't focus on nobody's else kid right now. I

called Dawn and she like, "if he come home, he come home" but she tired of dealing with him. Something about he'll be 18 next month and this ain't nothing new."

"She mad?"

"Sound like she just tired." Ronnie rubbed his right hand back and forth over his frayed cornrows. He hadn't bathed or eaten in two days. Davion was his only child. Having cared for him since he was three, it had been just the two of them for some time.

"I told you to watch D around him. He was too old. Knew too much and always got his hands in something. Got kicked out of school so much he stopped going."

"Yeah."

"I know that's probably the last thing you wanna hear right about now."

"Well if you know it…" Ronnie shrugged his shoulder. "Keep it to yourself."

"Sorry man. Clean up and let's get outta here. I gotta a few spots in mind to hit up. Somebody might know something."

"Do I look bad?"

"I wouldn't say all that. Just a little rough. Wish you would've put some clothes on and fixed up before you hit that camera. You know folk judging and all. Looking at you like another black thug and probably thinking the same about D."

"Let 'em think what they want. Unlike a lot of black dads around here I'm here… Dayum!" The wall felt the brunt of his frustration. "You know D don't know shit about this place or who he dealing with?"

"Yeah. I know. Come on man, you wasting time."

***

The boarded up row houses told the story of a Detroit that was headed towards bust. Sidewalks littered with trash, abandoned buildings and security bars covering every window of local establishments were a part of the regular landscape. In stark contrast, within a few miles were neighborhoods sprawling with middle and upper middle class residents who lived in nice homes in crime free zones.

"Turn right at the stop sign." Joe sat in the passenger seat and navigated Ronnie through the neighborhoods. The crime around Detroit wasn't relegated to what America knew-- cities with high-rise buildings occupied by mostly urban tenants. Instead, it was concentrated in areas with high vacancies and single-family homes. Joe knew the place like the back of his hand. There were some places he too was afraid to go. "Don't drive too slow. But don't drive too fast either. Just trying to check something out."

"Damn dude. You making me nervous. Don't act like Detroit is worse than Chicago."

"I'm not saying that. You know your city like I know mine. Just drive and let me do the talking."

"I hear ya." Ronnie conceded.

The high-rise projects could be seen from the Interstate. A cluster of what looked like 10 orange brick buildings were arranged in a U shape. They were notorious for the crime and poverty but also famous for the people who lived there over the years. Such greats as Diana Ross, Mary Wilson and Florence

When No One Came

Ballard also known as the Supremes once called Douglass Projects their home. "Pull up over there. Complex A." Joe pointed towards the driveway. "Wait here a minute and let me go up first."

"What's up?" Ronnie asked, uneasy. "You know something I don't know?"

"Yeah! That this is Dawn's son hangout. And unless you live here you really ain't got no business being here. So just chill and let me go up and ask a few questions. Stay here and don't be talking to nobody. Better yet recline the seat and just lay back."

"You crazy? I need to see what's going on."

"I'll be back in 15."

Leaning against the hood of the car Ronnie looked at his watch to note the time. A few boys played basketball. The balls clanged in and out of the net less rims as the boys yelled obscenities at each other. Midday meant they should have been in school. None of them looked older than 15. A girl pushing a stroller passed by with a toddler wearing nothing but a t-shirt, a diaper, and shoes following her. Who wants to live in this ghetto? Ronnie thought to himself. Moving was the first step, but couldn't be the last. This ordeal told him tat he needed to work on himself.

Joe could be seen walking across the courtyard in the distance talking to a group of people. Not longer after Ronnie heard him calling.

"Ronnie! Yo Ronnie!"

"What's up?" His feet carried him at record speed.

"They say Davion's been around here with Dawn's son. Ummmm Blocka."

He put his hands on his hips, dropped his head and walked a few steps away to compose himself. It felt like a ton of bricks had been lifted. At least he knew Davion wasn't dead and definitely had a lot of explaining to do. "Thanks man." He extended his hand. "When was the last time you saw them?"

"It was about 10 this morning. I was just getting back from dropping my moms off at work. I'm almost sure that's your son because he said he had just moved here from Chicago when I asked Blocka for a square."

"What he look like?"

"He 'bout this tall." The young man motioned with his had. "Low haircut. I think he got a birthmark or something on his forehead."

"Is this him?" Ronnie unfolded a piece of paper and showed him a picture of Davion."

"Yeah that's the shorty that was wit' Blocka."

"'Preciate that."

"Y'all can come up and wait if you want. Then again if Shorty ain't trying to come home right now, when he see your car, he gone get ghost again. Blocka be at everybody house so it might be a minute before you can catch him again."

Joe nodded his head. "He gotta point Ron. We can dip and come back or just stay posted down here. If he see you, you know he ain't gonna run."

"True. Thanks."

"No need. It's wild out here. Just glad to see shorty got somebody trying to see 'bout him. Blocka trouble. At the rate he

When No One Came

going he'll be dead soon. You don't want ya son around it."

"Yeah." Ronnie was short. His mind was racing. He missed the signs. Too busy running from the 9-5 to the 5-9 trying to put food on the table and help his aunt pay the bills until they got their own place. He didn't even know Bradley, or Blocka, as he was called, was a high school drop out-- having told him that he and Davion attended the same school. "I really appreciate you. We'll wait out here until they come back. You think they coming back?

"Yeah, yeah. Blocka girl lives over in B. You can see the apartment from here." Pointing in the direction of the complex. "Right there the second door on the left."

"Cool. Let's wait."

"Hope everything work out. You gotta square." The young man asked.

"Double for ya trouble." Ronnie handed him a pack of Newports.

***

The streetlights lit up the basketball court as night fell and still no signs of Davion or Bradley. It seemed like the night brought out more people, young and old and it became difficult to keep up with all the movement as Joe and Ronnie scanned the crowd for either or both boys. Loud music, smoke, talking, and the smell of beer filled the air. A couple of games of two on two were played back to back.

"Since we know where he at. You wanna come back tomorrow?" Joe was getting tired and restless.

"You can go. I ain't leaving without him."

"You know I can't leave you over here. The freaks come out at night."

"I ain't worried about that. Don't worry about me. I got this. Just 'preciate you for doing this much."

"This ain't nothing. We family. Momma already called me like twenty times." Joe laughed.

"Hold up, hold up." Tapping Joe on the shoulder Ronnie spotted his son. "Look over there in the cut. Right between A and B."

With excitement in his voice Joe agreed, "Hell yeah, that's them. How you wanna do this."

"Let me go around the back and come up and you go straight ahead. Bradley know you come over here so they might not think something's up and try to run. If they do I will be behind them."

"Cool, let's go." Joe responded eagerly.

It didn't take long to reach them and two other girls. Blocka was smoking a cigarette. After a few pulls he passed it to Davion.

"Davion!" Ronnie called out. "Have you lost your damn mind?" Before he could answer he had him hemmed up by his shirt collar. "Bradley don't even try it. Joe grab his little ass."

"Da…"

"Save that shit." Ronnie cut him off. He didn't know whether to hug him or whip him. "Y'all little girls need to go home." Passing Davion to Joe he grabbed Bradley.

"So this is how you do?" Ronnie stood face to face with Bradley. Sweating with white saliva in the corners of his mouth

When No One Came

Ronnie asked again. "So this is how we do?"

Attempting to break free from his grip. Bradley pulled away. "You don't want to even try it. I'm one second away from beating the hell out of you and I ain't even a violent person. You gonna tell me something."

"Dad, he didn't have nothing to do with this." Davion pleaded for his friend. Although his dad wasn't typically violent he knew that when he got mad it wouldn't be anything nice. "Come on. I'm ready to go."

"Davion, I'm advising you. And I'm only advising you once. Don't open your mouth again until I speak to you. Understood."

"Yes sir." He began to cry.

"And save the damn tears."

Now he had Bradley pushed against the side of the wall. A crowd started to gather. "Get your hands off of me!" Bradley tried to push his hands from his chest.

"That's not what I want to hear. What the hell where you thinking?"

"Hey, talk to your son. I ain't got nothing to do with it."

"You got everything to do with it. For two days now I sat at home pacing the damn floor wondering where he was and you got him out here in these streets. You got me acting a fool on TV."

"Don't blame me." It was obvious Bradley wasn't going to take ownership of Davion leaving home. "You got 'em. Now let me go."

Joe attempted to de-escalate the situation. He could see it going from zero to critical. "Yo, Ronnie. Let's get outta here. I understand you probably wanna be the shit outta Blocka but think about it. He's a minor, he ain't got shit to lose, and D needs you here not locked up behind no bars over this."

"This? This ain't just a this. My son coulda got killed, caught up some bullshit like robbing, drugs, who knows." Ronnie couldn't shake it.

"Dad, I'm alright. See. I made a mistake but I'm alright." Davion continued to plead except this time it was for his dad. If anything happened at that moment he wouldn't be able to forgive himself.

Hoping those were the words to his freedom Bradley pressed. "Dude listen to your son."

"Joe take him to the car. I'm on my way."

"Let's go to the car together."

"I'm coming." Ronnie wasn't budging. "It's gonna be alright."

"Man! Don't do nothing crazy." Joe held a tight grip on Davion as they walked towards the car.

"I'm gonna leave all this right here." Pulling a gun from his waistband he pressed it Bradley's head. "I welcomed you into my aunt's home. We broke bread with you. I trusted you around my son. I put a couple dollas in ya pocket and this is the thanks I get."

"I'm sorry. Don't shoot me. It ain't that serious." Bradley pleaded but he didn't cry.

"You don't tell me what's serious. My son is serious. Like I said I'mma leave it right here in these run down ass projects on this sidewalk. I pray that you get ya shit together before it's too late." He pressed the tip of the gun into Bradley's forehead. "I'm not going to shoot you...this time. But if I ever and I do mean ever see you around my son, my street, or anybody I care about again you can consider yourself dead." Ronnie stepped back pulled him off the wall and shoved him back into the wall hard enough that he hit his head.

Walking across the courtyard slowly he picked up his pace and shifted into a jog occasionally looking back over his shoulder. The news vans were gone and his street was quiet. Before walking into the house he pulled the missing poster from the street post and stared at it. His son was home but he couldn't help but think about the countless other sons that would never come home.

SHAKY GROUND

"We've come too far to just quit Tressa." Marissa pleaded.

"It's not about quitting. It's about safety. Some strange things are going on and you can't deny that."

"I'm not trying to but come on."

"I've been sleeping locked and loaded with a 38 special under my pillow and that shit is quite nerve wrecking." Tressa wasn't budging. "Remember Bob? What was that all about?"

"Gay is looking into it. Probably nothing."

"Nothing? Gay's been pissing a lot of folk off lately and maybe she's getting a little too comfortable. How can you be a private investigator and be everything but private?"

The sisters sat on the patio going back and forth about their next move. Tressa was getting antsy. The strange visits didn't make it any better. The debriefing from Florida was a bit overwhelming and now they were getting ready to start on another case of a missing black girl from South Carolina.

"Let's see it through. After these two if you still want to be done all together then it's cool. I think we owe it to Gay and ourselves to see it through. To be honest I think we owe to the families. And there really isn't any imminent danger." Marissa remained optimistic.

"Not now. Let Gay keep going. She might just meet her match and piss some really important person off. Let us, the Hawks, keep going."

"This is the work we do and that comes with the territory."

"Uh noooo, it's not what we do. But I hear you and will think about it." Tressa reclined back in the chair and massaged her temples. The weather was kinder today. A light breeze blew across her face.

"It's going to be ok."

"I hear you Rissa. Will you refresh the lemonade and get the files we are supposed to be going through?"

"Files are on the tray table next to you. Give me a sec on the other." Being careful to not rock the boat she obliged.

The ladies were working two active missing child cases and assisting Gay with closing out the case with Parker Monroe, Mr. CEO. After the trip to LA, there seemed to be more to Mr. Monroe that cheating with his wife. The two men he worked with were involved in something that had a long paper trail and quite a few hands involved. They were still trying to figure out what the Mayor's role was in all of it.

"Rissa!" Tressa called into the house. "Bring the corkboard with you and some push pins." Thumbing through the files she pulled out all the photos and began organizing them on the table.

"Here ya go. What's up?"

"Not sure yet. Just trying to figure out how all the players are connected. Something just doesn't feel right about it."

With the corkboard propped against the wall, Tressa put pictures of the Queen and King at the top. The Queen being the Mayor and the King, Parker Monroe. To the side of the King she placed a picture of Mrs. Monroe and directly under she placed pictures of the two men they met with in LA.

Marissa stood back and watched her put the pieces of the growing puzzle together. The business line rang breaking her train of thought. "Ms. Radcliffe." She had decided to use her maiden name while moonlighting for Gay after finding out that Monroe Parker was one of the individuals she was hired to investigate.

"Hi Marissa. David James."

"Oh! Hi David. What do you have for me?"

Marissa had become secretly obsessed with the Parker Monroe case-- so much so that she had asked Gay to include her on all surveillance and meetings about him. She couldn't fathom a man so powerful being so dirty. Regardless of the fact that since the beginning of time many a powerful man had been taken down by the love of money and/or women.

"I think you're on to something. Something really big. It looks like you aren't the only one interested in Mr. Parker Monroe and his Ms. Kimberly LaSalle."

"Go on."

"Well, after some digging around, I found that the IRS has a tax evasion probe going on and the gentlemen you inquired about are involved in everything from illegal gambling to prostitution. They are connected with some pretty big folk, from politicians to high ranking law enforcement officials, from the east coast to the west coast."

"Really?" Marissa wanted to know more, having hired him to dig into Mr. Monroe's background. David's firm had the bandwidth to take unconventional measures to get information about certain individuals without raising any red flags. "Can you scan the file over to me? I'm particularly interested in the two men. You can overnight the rest."

"Sure. Word of caution. Be careful. This just may be too big for you ladies."

"Noted. Thanks David and I will be in touch."

"No problem. You should have the file in about 10 mins."

Tressa had stopped organizing the board to listen in on the conversation. "What was that about?"

"Well, Mr. Monroe is up to a lot of no good. Waiting on the file to come over so we can close some of these gaps." Pointing at the board she smirked.

"Ok while we are waiting on that. Quick update on the Mabrey and Langston cases."

"You or me?" Marissa asked.

"I was offering since you missed the last meeting."

"Cool."

"Mabrey- both bikes that were found were sent to the state crime lab and analyzed for fingerprints, fibers, and any possible fluids. The weather probably eliminated any possibility of fluids.

There is a backlog but Detective Graham was trying to get the processing on the priority list. Should have something back in a few weeks. There is a little positivity though." This was a case that was growing on Tressa but was more Olivia's baby. She had begun to have weekly phone calls with Mrs. Mabrey and each week she learned more and more not only by Josalyn but the family. The Mabrey family had become hers.

"What's the positivity?"

"The local lab was able to lift some preliminary prints off of both bikes so they are running those through the database. Hopefully we will get a match." There was no secret to Tressa's vested interest in this case.

"That's good news and the Langston case?"

"They are continuing to question the students about that night. Still don't have a license plate to identify the car but they do know who the driver was. We'll be heading down there in a few weeks and knock on some doors."

"Moving right along." Marissa nodded. "And press?"

"Olivia and Gay are working a few angles. Gay has called in a few favors but she's still waiting to hear back. Will make a note to follow up with them tomorrow."

The ice in the lemonade had melted but it was still refreshing. Tressa held the glass to her neck and forehead to allow the condensation on the outside to cool her off. She thought to herself that the detective work wasn't so bad. It was all the other stuff that came with it.

"Bingo." Marissa moved her arm in a motion like pulling a lever on a slot machine. "I got mail! Hold on let me run and print this. Hey babes." She stopped to kiss Jonathan.

"Hey Sis!" Jonathan had come home and had been standing behind the screen of the patio watching, and ladies were so into the conversation that they had not noticed. "Hey Boy! Looking good."

"Thanks lady. You not looking too bad yourself." He smiled and gave Tressa a nod of approval.

"Come give me a hug. I haven't seen you in a month of Sundays." Beckoning for him to come out. "We need to do better."

Scooping her up around her waist he squeezed hard. "You right about that. I see you two are really taking this thing serious."

"You can say that."

"Is that a good thing or bad thing."

"It's all good." Tressa dared not tell Jonathan about the guy stopping by the bar.

"Well don't let me interrupt. You two hungry? I can hook something up." Cooking was Jonathan's favorite pass time and he could burn.

"You're not interrupting." Marissa stole another kiss. "I can eat."

"Me too." Tressa chimed in.

"I can cook! I'll hook y'all up."

"Thanks babe." Jonathan was definitely a Godsend. He took very good care of Marissa and the rest of the family, and for that, she was thankful; although it took several years down the line to realize just how special he was. Smiling, she watched him walk into the kitchen. "Okay here we go." Pointing at the older gentlemen. "This bad boy is Mr. Frederick Risner, CEO and founder of Risner Communications. He has been in the telecom/mass media industry for over 20 years."

"And how is he connected to Mr. Monroe?"

"Hold your horses. We're going to get to that. At least I hope."

"And bad boy number two?" Tressa pointed to the younger one with the S- Curl in his head.

"That bad boy would be Rick Norwood aka Pretty Ricky aka Slick Rick depending on the audience." Marissa cracked herself up.

"Girl stop. Are those his aliases for real?"

"For real. For real." Marissa hollered. "Girl!"

"And what does he do on paper because looking at the picture he got some other ish going on."

"He is a real estate developer on paper. But it looks like he runs numbers and girls for Risner."

Tressa pulled the pictures down and jotted a few notes on them. "Give me that file over there. The blue one."

"What's up?" Marissa asked out of curiosity.

"I remember reading something about Gay overheard them talking about getting ready for the convention season."

"She did."

"This can't be what I think it is." Tressa shook her head in disbelief.

"I think it is what you think it is."

The smell of burgers on the Foreman Grill lingered through the patio. "Ladies, burgers up in 20."

"Hold that thought. Damn! This is big. Will you pick this up while I go help J? We can pick up tomorrow."

"Not tomorrow but in a day or two. I have some things I need to take care of... like the spa,"

Marissa gave her a high five. "I know that's right. Self preservation is key."

Tressa reclined in the chair and looked up at the night sky and spoke aloud. "Lord I don't have a clue about why you have me here in the place, messing around with this stuff but whatever the reason I pray that whatever your will is it will be done. Ummm umm um." She let out a light chuckle. "I'm going to go with it for now." That was her way of bargaining. Still a little conflicted she felt better knowing she wasn't alone and the promise of being able to walk away whenever was in the forefront of her mind.

JANE DOE

The fresh smell of brewing coffee permeated the air coupled with the sound of a percolating pot. An early freeze had come over the city although old man winter had yet to arrive. A typical Sunday called for coffee with a touch of French vanilla creamer, bible reading at the kitchen table, with a little gospel music playing in the background. Wrapped in a pink and yellow housecoat Ms. Langston poured her a cup, grabbed two pieces of toast, and sat facing the window. Three stick trees stood lonely. All the birds had flown Deep South for the winter. The garden had frosted over for now. She smiled to herself thinking about how Dynasty had just the right amount of country in her bones. That country came from her dad's side. She couldn't wait for the tomatoes and cucumbers to be ready. *The blood that Jesus shed for me way back on Calvary...*

"The blood that gives me strength from day to day will never lose its power." Singing along just above a whisper Ms. Langston tapped her foot slowly to the beat. "It reaches to the highest mountain and it flows to the lowwwwest valley."

Her hands rubbed the cover of the burgundy leather bible. The edges were beginning to fold and the leather was wearing away

When No One Came

at the creases. There was a remnant of a few gold letters that once spelled Dynasty Langston. The thin grade paper that the text was printed upon crinkled under her fingers as she thumbed through the pages searching for just the right passage of scripture to minister to her. The first passage she turned to was Isaiah 41 and 10, which read, *Do not fear, for I am with you; do not be dismayed, for I am your God. I will strengthen you, I will help you, yes, I will uphold you with my righteous right hand.* "Yes Lord." She proclaimed. Sitting at the table she mediated on the particular text and read it aloud twice more. Each time reading slower and pausing between sentences.

"Do not fear, for I am with you; do not be dismayed, for I am your God." She paused. "I will strengthen you, I will help you." Pausing again she spoke as to be speaking directly to God. "Yes, I can use your strength Father God."

"Ms. Langston can you meet us at the station?" The voice on the other end asked.

Gripping the phone paralyzed by fear she hung up without responding and sat back at the table. She continued to keep her mind on comforting scriptures. Turning to Philippians 4 and 6, one of her favorite verses, she raised her voice as loud as she could and read it out loud. *Be anxious for nothing, but in everything, by prayer and supplication with gratitude, make your requests known to God.* "You already know, but I'm going to ask again, please bring Dynasty home safely. I miss her dearly." The coffee was no longer warm and the toast was now cold. An hour had passed and the phone rang a few more times.

"Olivia Marston."

"Olivia this is Ms. Langston. I need you girls to come over right away. There's been a call for me to come to the station."

"We have a few more neighbors to question and we will be right there." Olivia replied hoping that a hint of assurance came through her voice. This side of their work was still new, unsettling, and at times frightening. Just as these emotions hit her came the feelings of anger and hurt. Angry that no one seemed to give a damn, and that without money or status there were simply no answers to be gotten. Hurt, she couldn't help but empathize with a parent although she was childless. It was only human to feel for a parent who didn't know the whereabouts or condition of the person they were charged with caring for, keeping safe, and providing for. Injury was always added to insult for those single parenting. They were being punished for choosing a job over a life of poverty.

"Thank you. I will get dressed." "This ain't my battle," looking up at the ceiling she grimaced fighting back the tears."

Another hour had passed before she was completely dressed. If she was going to see something or get some bad news she was going to be well dressed for it. A maroon dress and flesh tone stockings were paired with maroon and black shoes with spool heels.

Startled by a rapid knock at the door, the chair Ms. Langston was sitting in almost tilted over. She pulled the curtain back slightly to see two women on the porch.

"Olivia and Marissa. Come on in. Would you like something to drink?" She began to employ the stall tactics.

"No thank you, Ms. Langston. You called to say that you received a call to come to the station."

"Yes."

"What else was said?"

"I didn't get anymore details. I hung up." She replied nonchalantly. The highs and lows of her tone revealed a deeper angst and fear.

"Where are the other ladies?"

"They were following up on leads in the Lancaster. They are about an hour away and will be heading this way. We can wait for them or we can go now."

"What do you think? Do you think they found her?"

Unable to look Ms. Langston in the eyes and provide her with an answer Olivia looked past her and responded, "there could be a break in the case."

"Why couldn't they just stop by and tell me that?"

"We are uncertain of what is needed. It's only assumption from past experience." Marissa lied. There had not been that much past experience. They were working more cases but running into a lot of opposition. Having a license to be a private investigator was nothing like being a detective. Skill sets may be similar but the credentials varied and a license garnered you very little respect. Law enforcement really didn't see the agency as being partners working towards a common goal. "Would you like to go now?"

Hesitating, "Yes. I guess the other ladies can meet us there."

Several months had passed before the ladies could actually get on the ground there for a period of time although they had been in touch with Chief Buckner on occasion. He had been willing to allow them to do their work from the sidelines but unlike Detective Graham he kept a very tight lid on evidence and information. Apparently, the last story ran did not show him in a favorable light so he was out to prove a point. That mindset didn't help the progression of the case.

***

More cars than usual packed the parking lot of the small police station. A lone news car parked at an angle in front. The building was even less inviting as the maple trees on either side were nothing but trunk and roots. In the summer and early fall the station resembled a small brick house. The only things that gave it away were the occasional squad car, signage, and glass doors.

"Sit tight. Let me go in." Olivia took the lead.

"Sure." Marissa turned to engage Ms. Langston in small conversation as a mere distraction although it was obvious her mind and thoughts rested with whatever was taking place behind those doors."

Olivia appeared after a few minutes and beckoned them from the steps. The vapors from her breathing could be seen as she exhaled into the cold air.

"Ms. Langston go on in. We will be there shortly." Puzzled Ms. Langston didn't offer a verbal response but nodded.

Pulling Marissa to the side to debrief her, Olivia held the door open with the free hand for Ms. Langston. Olivia's eyes gleamed with tears. That could have only meant one thing.

"We were too late."

"What?"

"There is nothing being said but the movement inside is a telltale sign."

"Wait did anyone say anything or are you going on a hunch."

"We were too late." This time her voice shook loudly.

"Damn."

"Pull yourself together. Let's go in." Marissa remained stoic.

Phones rang from wall to wall. A reporter stood by the main desk with a notepad in hand and a cell phone to her ear. There was very little talk but lots of movement. A meeting was happening on one side of the room. Looking around for Mrs. Langston the two spotted her in the chief's office.

"We are here with Ms. Langston."

"One second please let me speak with Chief Buckner."

They could see the officer talking to the chief and then Ms. Langston before summoning them to the office. Ms. Langston sat facing the chief. Any sound was muffled as the door and windows acted as a barrier. The movement outside the office was still fluid but more eyes seemed to be tuned into what was happening inside the office.

"Ms. Langston are you ok?"

Turning to face Olivia, her face had lost any color and tears flowed like a river. Wringing her hands she directed her. "Ask Chief Buckner why we are here." Olivia paused and looked in his direction.

"Yes?"

"There has been a body discovered. It matches Dynasty's description. There was one shoe found and some clothing in a bag. It matches the dress she was last seen wearing but she's wearing something different now. We would like to go over to the county morgue and have Ms. Langston make a positive identification."

"Where? How?" Olivia fought to contain herself.

"We don't know and It's just too early to tell. Even more important this is an active murder investigation and we can't jeopardize a case."

"Murder?" Marissa spoke up.

"We are going to treat this as a murder until we see otherwise."

"I promised her I wouldn't be late." Ms. Langston's broke through.

"Take your time." Chief Buckner passed the tissue box around.

***

The hallways of Mercy General were quiet and cold. The walk to the wing were the morgue was located was akin to walking down death row. It was a certain fate that lied ahead and the slower you walked one could only hope that meeting that fate would be delayed. Peering into every passed room, whatever was happening inside each of them was a blur. Gay and Tressa, having arrived ahead of time waited on their arrival.

Her feet weighing heavy like bricks, Ms. Langston's pace slowed drastically as they rounded the final corner. After all, she worked here, so she knew the fastest and the longest routes but opted for the latter. For that moment she had cried all the tears she had. Her mouth was dry and she couldn't speak. Standing on either side of her, Gay and Olivia were human crutches. At this point they were carrying her.

"You don't have to do this right now."

Shaking her head. She stopped and looked towards Tressa and uttered, "It's time. It's time."

"We are here every step of the way."

Having made their way to the doorway, Ms. Langston was guided to a bench immediately outside.

"Rest a while." Gay suggested.

"It's time." She refused to sit. "I'm ready."

Gay opened the door and lying on the steel table was a body under a white sheet. The feet were uncovered but tag less. The coroner called Ms. Langston to the head of the table. Olivia held her underneath her arms but could feel her weight buckling underneath her.

"Marissa."

Holding her up on the other side, Ms. Langston's breathing became heavy and labored. Tressa stayed outside. The women had never seen a dead body before. They had never been in this situation before, near death unbeknownst to them, but not at death's door.

"Ms. Langston do you know who this is?" Pulling back the sheet just enough to reveal the face the coroner asked.

"Dynasty! My baby." She wailed loudly as though she too was dying.

***

"Chief Buckner. Do you have a minute to speak with us?" Gay asked.

"Sure."

"What happened? Where did you find her?"

The ladies stood in the hallway of Mercy General forming a semi circle around him. Ms. Langston had been admitted and was under sedation. They had not been in town for a day and were devastated by the news. There were too many unanswered questions. They knew that because it was an ongoing investigation only so much could be divulged.

"She was found about 20 minutes from here."

"How?"

"One of the boys she was last seen just cracked. Whatever happened weighed so heavily on him that he confided his dad who called a lawyer and the lawyer called us." Detective Graham shook his head. "She was right under our nose for at least a week."

Tressa interrupted. "Are you saying that she was alive for at least a week? Twenty minutes from here? And you all still couldn't find her?"

"I'm not sure what I'm saying. If you ladies would keep this right here." He pointed to the floor. "This is still pretty much an active investigation and we plan to find and prosecute every single person involved to the fullest extent of the law. However long and whatever it takes."

"Damn that sounds good." Olivia remarked with disgust in her voice. "Why couldn't you use that same vigor at first? You all dropped the ball and I hope that you all are investigated and prosecuted."

"For what?"

"You have blood on your hands." Emotions ran high as

When No One Came

Olivia pointed blame.

"Wait a minute Olivia." Gay stepped in front of her. "We are allies remember. Now is not the time to get distracted. To get up in your emotions. Now is definitely not the time to point fingers when we ourselves don't know all the facts. At this point we might not know until there is an arrest and trial." She continued to be the voice of reason.

"Whatever." Olivia stormed off. "You can have this. I'm done with these wild goose chases." Deep down inside her biggest fear was the same thing happening with Josalyn. It had been almost two years and nothing. Dynasty had only been missing for 7 months and she was dead. Emotionally she would not be able to handle it, body or not.

"Olivia." Tressa called after her.

"Let her go." Gay spoke firmly. "Give her some space. She'll be ok."

"Damn, can you turn off the switch and stop acting like a robot for once? We know you all hard. A bad ass. But damn. We have a woman here who has just found out her daughter has been killed."

"I get that."

"Well act like it."

Chief Buckner stepped back and rested against the wall. "If you gotta blame somebody I will take it for now. I'm going to make it right one way or the other. There is no need to fight and get mad at one another. You ladies are doing a good thing. At least you care."

"Caring obviously isn't enough." Marissa who had been

quiet the entire time finally spoke. "Come on y'all pull it together." Olivia was out of site and Tressa was soon to be. Marissa caught a glimpse of her coat as she rounded the corner at the end of the opposite hall.

"Y'all? It looks like it's just you and me." Gay spoke devoid of emotion.

"I see." Marissa would have thought she was crazy but understood her all to well. Gay the psychology major rarely used what she learned and knew on her own self. She never took a dose of her own medicine. "I'm going to stop by Ms. Langston's room and then catch up with you all at the hotel. I can grab a taxi over there.

"I'll go with you. Chief Buckner don't be so hard on yourself. One thing for sure it will all come out in the wash. If you acted too slowly, without aggression, with aggression. Whatever it is and I pray you find piece with that." Gay reached out and grabbed Marissa around the shoulder and they walked together.

HOLD THEM OR FOLD THEM

Marissa, with her feet buried in the corners of the overstuffed sofa, lie back resting her arms over her head. She was dreading the much-needed talk with Jonathan, but things had reached their tipping point. A point she thought they would never reach. It's through sickness and health, for better or for worse, "until death," right? Looking around the room she couldn't help but be proud of their accomplishments as a team. They were enjoying the fruits of their labor. Engineering had been good to them. The unusual ceiling pattern illuminated warm hues from behind the blocks. Heat resistant windows stretched from corner to corner allowing plenty of sunlight to enter while blocking the intense heat the geography offered.

"Rissa?" Jonathan called out before he could get over the threshold good.

"Yes honey."

"Can you come here for a sec to help me with the bags."

Bags? Marissa began to think that maybe the talk wouldn't be so bad. Jonathan's stop at the grocery store could perhaps mean a truce. "Hi honey." Leaning in for a kiss. "Thanks for doing that. The refrigerator was on empty."

"Yeah, I remember a time when that was never an issue. Now you seem to be pre-occupied with saving the world."

"That's not really fair."

Handing her the bags he had in his hand, he replied, "What's this really about? Either it's fair or it's not."

"It's not really fair means that yeah I get that I've been slacking around here. I've been slacking on us. But I need your support and understanding. I know it's difficult. "

"Let me get the rest of the bags. We can talk later. Better yet let's go for a run if you feel up to it and then I will cook us dinner." It was sounding more and more like a truce to Marissa."

"Sure, I will put these things away and change clothes."

***

Their subdivision offered every amenity that a family could ask for with the exception of shopping and a grocery store. Nonetheless a work out facility, spa, pool, a few dining areas, and walking trails were all within a 10-mile radius. Running was one of the many things the two had in common and they always enjoyed each other's company during that time even after the college. From time to time they would race each other to see who still had it.

"Let's catch the longer trail."

"Somebody has some energy to burn I see." Marissa joked.

"Yeah I would rather burn it in other places but I need help doing that."

"That's low."

"Maybe so but leaving your husband high and dry for your friends or this new found career is even lower."

"It's not a new found career. We are working to help find our brown babies."

"For how long? There will always be another one."

"I agree but maybe we can bring more awareness to what's going on and hopefully get more people involved, interested, and caring."

The conversation was in full effect before they could finish stretching. The two had conflict resolution down to a science. It was rare that tension was allowed to build to an intolerable space. Yet, this time was different. There were so many elements to the conflict that tackling them took not only open and honest listening but also a different level of transparency. Marissa trumped protocol this time around by discussing her involvement with Gay's agency after the fact. It was an ask for forgiveness later kind of move. It was a selfish move because of the unforeseen danger.

Setting his timer after one last leg stretch, "Ready?"

"Sure. Slow and steady wins the race." Marissa winked. She did not want Jonathan to be upset with her. But she understood his feelings came from a place of feeling deceived- shut out. They came from a place of concern not only for her but also for all of the ladies. All of them had been friends since college so they were family now.

"Do you really understand why I'm mad?" Will you at admit this thing has caused you to put us on the backburner? If not for being in between contracts at the job I wonder if this would affect that as well."

"Yes, Jonathan I do understand and I owe you an apology. I apologize. What would you like me to do? I will quit."

"I accept your apology. But I know you better than that. If you signed up for this It's because one, you care, and two, you are just that "ride or die" kind of friend."

"Yikes, I don't like that analogy."

"Yeah that was a bit..."

"Much." Marissa completed his sentence. "You know me too well."

"It's ok babe. Not all good but ok. If it's not too much to ask, tell me what's going on. Let me help if I can. Gay told me you were out there shooting your ass off. I'm sure you can handle yourself ok, but be vigilant at all times, especially on your stake outs. That's what you call it right?"

"Funny. No we call it surveillance mister."

"Well be careful on your surveillance and if it gets too hot, leave and don't be afraid to call the police."

"Yes boss."

"You got that right. I am the boss." He laughed.

Without realizing it they had run 5 miles with another 5 to get back to the main street.

"Seriously know your limits and don't be afraid to say when. We still have babies to make."

"Babies?" They had tabled this conversation until later. The later had come with them having purchased a home, stability in careers, paid off debt, and savings amassed. All the contingencies had been checked off.

"Yes Marissa. It's time."

"Give me a year."

"A year and nothing more."

***

"Go and grab your shower. I'll get dinner started." Jonathan patted her on the behind and pushed her gently in the direction of the bedroom.

"I wanted to help." Marissa turned and gave him a sad face.

"You still can. Get your shower get comfortable come back and take over and then I will grab my shower. We can do the old switcheroo." He winked.

Planting a long kiss on his lips. "That'll work. Be back shortly."

To Marissa's surprise Jonathan had drawn a bubble bath, lit candles all around the garden tub. There were no rose petals or wine per usual. Just a simple relaxing bath. She smiled and stepped out of her clothes. Bending down to pick them up she could see Jonathan walk in behind her. "I got 'em." Get in and relax. Take your time."

"Awe babes." When did you do this?"

"While you were talking to the neighbor. Doesn't take long to run some water, add a few bath beads, and to light a few candles here and there." He answered with modesty.

"This is true but I think you're underestimating on the few

candles. Let me see, I count 5, 8, 12, 20 dang J., 25 candles, really?

"Anything for you."

"I know and appreciate it.'

"Get in the tub if you appreciate it." He laughed and held her hand as she stepped up and over. "Let me get your music going and I will be back to check on you."

"Sweet man you are."

Marissa sank back in the tub with her head resting on the spa pillow. The deep soaking Jacuzzi tub was designed with a headrest on both ends. The jets sprayed at low speed offering a gentle massage. Sounds of saxophones, trumpets and trombones filled the room. Her feet swayed under water with the beat of the music. Squeezing water over her face and head she sighed. She felt the love. The light from the candles danced off her eyes before she fully closed them.

Ambien had become her confidant, lulling her to sleep for the past 4 months. With every closed eye came a vision of Dynasty Langston's lifeless body lying on a cold steel table. She thought about Jonathan wanting a baby. She was ready as well and had stopped taking her birth control months ago, but the added stress on her body and mind made conceiving difficult. Four visits later, the obstetrician had exhausted all tests. She was fine. There was nothing medically wrong that was preventing them from getting pregnant.

"Relax ma'am." She spoke to herself sternly. "You are in the now. Enjoy it. Let tomorrow take care of itself." Closing her eyes completely she lay back, just being.

"Dinner is served." Jonathan opened the bathroom door.

When No One Came

Peeking over the side of the tub she could see a single rose, a bottle of wine, and two glasses on the table in their nook. The bedroom area was especially designed like a bed and breakfast and the two often ate breakfast or impromptu dinners here. It was close enough but far away enough from the sleeping area.

"You are showing out Mr."

"Is that what you call it now? I guess I too have been slacking."

"No babes. You have been perfect."

"Dry off. Get comfortable and I will be there in 2 minutes." Jonathan had changed clothes.

"You took a shower already?"

"Yep, in the guest bath."

"I should've known. You don't miss a beat." Marissa joked while drying off.

The table tent read Pan-Seared Scallops on Linguine with Tomato-Cream Sauce. A bottle of Chardonnay from Château de Beaucastel was the pairing of choice. The simple but elegant layout exuded love.

"Thank you so much Jonathan." Marissa smiled widely.

"You're welcomed beautiful."

They ate, talked, laughed, and didn't take anything else too seriously for the rest of the night. Jonathan stood up, extending his hand. Marissa accepted as he led her to the bed. It had been a while since they were intimate. Yes, they had sex, but it was rushed and lazy. Tonight, they took it back to intimacy. Taking the time to enjoy each other.

UNNECESSARY ROUGHNESS

"Gay Thibodeaux?" The gruffness of the caller's voice caused her to turn the car radio down to hear clearly. "Gay Thibodeaux?"

"Yes, may I ask who's calling?"

"You should know?"

"If I knew, there wouldn't be a need to ask. Now, may I ask again, who's calling and how may I help you?"

"You shouldn't be surprised. Did you think it would be long before I called?"

"I'm not surprised just unaware of who this is. And the sooner you identify yourself the sooner we can get down to business... if needed." She maintained her composure.

"Why so serious?" The caller chuckled.

Gay hung up the phone. The anonymous nature of the call did not allow her to block the call or trace it. She noted the time, as this was the first time someone actually addressed her. The calls had been happening since the strange visit from Bob. Her line was set up to reject anonymous calls; however the caller had a device to bypass the feature so his calls came through. Sometimes three or four times in one day. Other days there was nothing. Nonetheless, it left her feeling on edge all the time. The other ladies had received a few of the calls as well but not to the extent that she had.

The phone rang again, and Gay answered without looking at the caller ID. Immediately she went into a rant. "I'm not sure who you are and I'm not sure what you want but I will tell you this isn't it!"

"You're right about that. I prefer men. Tall, dark, and handsome with a little thickness at that." The person on the other end burst into laughter. "Gay, this is Tressa. What's going on?"

"You play to much wench!"

"What's up for real?" Tressa was becoming concerned.

"So the coward that has been calling us and just holding the phone finally got the balls to speak up."

"How do you know it's the same person?

"You're right. I just assumed since all the calls didn't start until after that goofy ass looking Bob character showed up."

"Gotcha. What did he say?"

"He didn't say much of nothing but tried to play some mind games. I hung up on him."

"Did his voice sound familiar?"

"Never heard it in my life. Just rough as hell."

"Are you okay?"

"You know me. I'm good."

"How did I know you were going to say that?" Tressa shook her head and pulled the phone from her ear. It pained her that Gay walked around with this tough girl persona 24/7/365. It was cool to be strong, but humans aren't built that way. Pipes under pressure all the time burst. "I hear ya. So where are you now?"

"I'm headed to pick up Naja and I guess we'll catch a movie or something. I've been going like crazy and she hasn't complained one time."

"That doesn't tell me where you are." Tressa asked again. It wasn't like she could really do something but at least she would know where to send the police if something went down.

"Dang you the po-po now?"

"You definitely trying to make me one. I'm a hawk and I'm hawking your ass." Tressa couldn't resist. "That was good I know. You ain't gotta tell me."

"It was alright! You soooo silly, I promise! All jokes aside I'm on Del Ray Ave. I'm gonna make a quick stop to pick up some pictures from The Imaging Hub and then I 'm headed directly to get Naja from school. Is that enough detail for you or should I give you time stamps for each stop as well?"

"All that ain't even necessary but I do thank you. Just call me or text when you make it to the movies if that's not too much to ask.

"It's not. Thanks for the concern Chica and the laughs. I think you may have found your second calling."

"Funny but negative. That humorous side is something that just grew on me. Gotta keep the kids laughing instead of crying.

When No One Came

You know they not trying to see the big bad dentist. Talk to ya later."

"Tressss.." She hung up the phone before Gay could ask the reason for her call.

The phone rang again. "I was just going to ask…"

"Ask me." The voice on the other interrupted.

"How may I help you?" It wasn't Tressa as she assumed. but Gay stood firm in her demeanor.

"I'm glad you asked. My client knows you have been following him and he doesn't take it to kindly."

"Well maybe your client shouldn't be doing things that would cause for me to follow him." She returned with sass.

"His business is just that. His business."

"Well, we all know what my business is. Folk like him keep me in business."

Undeterred by her straightforwardness, the caller came back with a little more force. "We can do this the easy way or the hard way. You see my business is similar to yours and I just may be a little craftier. Ehh an even better word. Let's say skillful. It's not often that the hunter is hunted is it?"

"Use whatever word you would like. I've heard you. I will back off when what I've been hired to do is finished. As you both will see, I don't scare easily."

"Does Naja?"

Gay pulled over immediately to the nearest curb, jumped out of her car with the phone still to her ear, and looked around, visibly shaken in a matter of minutes. That one question had taken her strength. This person had crossed the line. If he knew her daughter's name she wondered what more he knew. If he was following her now? How long had he been following her before now? He had the upper hand- a clear visual into her life. "Listen you piece of shit. I don't know who you are. Who hired you? Or what the hell you want but when it comes to my child. All bets are off and I will burn your ass." She refused to let her voice show that she was afraid although she paced from the front of the car to the back. By this time she was on the side nearest the curb continuing to look around and holding the phone tightly.

"I got your attention now I see."

"Damn right. Now what do you want?"

"It's simple. Everything that you have on my client. Turn it over and what can't be turned over, like computer files, need to be permanently deleted."

"I have a lot of clients."

"None as high profile and wealthy as this one."

"Bullshit."

"So that's a no."

"I didn't say no. Who is the client?" She played hardball.

Continuing to look around she was unable to see anyone remotely close to someone that could possibly be following her. Cars zipped up and down the street. A few rubbernecked but didn't stop. Just as she stepped off the curb to walk to the driver's side a black Camaro zoomed by so close it almost side swiped her car. It was only a few inches from sending her to meet her maker. The hood of the car broke her fall. Pieces of her broken cell phone scattered across the pavement. A tinted cover obscured the car's tag. The window tint coupled with the speed of the car made it virtually impossible to see the driver. She cringed from the pain of her elbow hitting the hood. Needing to act quickly she rushed to get her personal cell phone from the car.

"Mariiiisssa answer the phone. Come on." She spoke out loud hitting the steering wheel. "Mariiisssaaa. Shit."

"What's up Booskie?"

"I need you to run to the school and pick up Naja and take her to your house." Gay yelled frantically.

"Calm down. What's wrong?"

"Just do it and I will call you later."

"No ma'am we don't get down like that and you know it. I'm on my way to get her but I need for you to tell me what the hell is going on?" Marissa asked anxiously.

"I will. Call me when you all have made it your house." Hanging up the phone Gay turned on her hazard lights and sped off. Marissa called back to back with Gay ignoring the call. She had no time to explain how she had been infiltrated. The entire idea or legacy of her being the best at which she did was unraveling before her eyes.

Two police cars where sitting in the driveway when she got home, having called them on the way, reporting that a neighbor had called her to say there was a suspicious car at her house. She lied but needed some protection. Her gun was home and the way the anonymous person used his car as a weapon she was not going to take any chances.

"Ms. Thibodeaux?"

"Yes officers. Thank you for coming so quickly." She feigned distress.

"Just doing our job. Serving and protecting."

"I appreciate you all. Did you have a chance to check the perimeter?"

"Perimeter?" Obviously not familiar with Gay and her line of work they were confused by the usage of that word. "Law enforcement?"

"Television." She laughed softly.

"That's pretty cool. But yeah we checked the area, front and back. It's all clear. Would you like us to go inside and have a look around?"

"Yes, if you don't mind."

"Hang out here and we will be back as soon as possible."

"Take your time." Gay sat on the hood of the car and waited for the officers. "Hey you got her?"

"Yeah, now tell me what's going on."

"Rissa the anonymous caller is now making visits."

"What do you mean making visits and what caller?"

"The caller I told you about. The same one I think called y'all. He called a few times and then he tried to run me over."

"Wait a minute. Slow down. You're not making sense."

"I don't have time for this right now. Just keep Naja with

you. Call Tressa and Olivia. Get the files you have in your possession and get ready to meet me in about an hour. See if Jonathan can watch Naja. I will call you back with the location."

"Where are you now?"

"Home with the police."

"Police? You're scaring me now."

"Don't be. Call you back in an hour or less."

The street was empty. Gay was expecting a few of the older neighbors to be outside by now, with not one but two police cars being parked in front of her house. She walked to the mailbox curious as to if anything was inside but also afraid to open it for fear of a bomb or something. The notion was far fetched but anything was possible right about now. She had been considering a move into a gated community over the past year for safety reasons, but had not found the time to contact a realtor to begin the search. That was her next order of business. Her current community was settled and nice and relatively crime free with the occasional egging by wayward teens. She stood on the curb waiting for a black Camaro to pull up, lower his window, and shoot her. Her mind was running wild, absent of reason.

"Ms. Thibodeaux." The officer called. "Ms. Thibodeaux." This time touching her on the shoulder and startling her. "I apologize. Didn't mean to scare you. Everything looks fine inside. If there isn't anything else we will leave now. Or would you like us to speak to the neighbor who called you?"

"Ohhh." She had almost forgotten about that lie. "Oh no. That won't be necessary. I will stop by and chat with her. You know how the elderly can be. Any little thing will alarm them."

"Those are the best kind of neighbors."

"I agree. Thank you again for your time." Shaking their hands she thanked them again.

Although the officers gave an all clear she was still quite tense. Her two story brick home had been her safe haven for 4 years. She never had a break in or unexpected guest. She didn't entertain beyond her close family and friends. That was the downside of being an investigator. She pulled her car into the garage and hurriedly went inside activating the alarms and cameras. Every angle of the house was under surveillance. Tipping from room to room she left nothing uninspected from the closets to the drawers to under the beds. There was one thing about a homeowner, they knew the placement of everything in the home and could readily spot when something had been moved.

"Hey! What time is it?"

"You said you would call us within the hour. What's taking you so long?" Marissa asked agitated.

"I was just packing clothes for Naja. She's flying to her dad's tonight."

"Is it that serious?"

"I rather be safe than sorry. I'm going to text the address to Olivia and Tressa. I'm going to run by there to see Naja and we can ride together. I will fill you all in at the same time. Too exhausted and too much to be repeating."

"I guess. How long?"

"Leaving now." Gay tucked the phone in her pocket before pulling out the gun box. She put on the holster and tucked the gun inside with an extra clip.

***

The office building was one of the tallest in the city. Gay had been renting the space for the last 6 months, having decided that she would take the firm to the next level and operate in full capacity in the search and rescue of missing children after the death of Dynasty Langston. She felt she owed Dynasty that much. The windows facing the hall where covered with paper, sheet rock and plastic were everywhere. Half of the office was ready while the other half was still being renovated. The ladies met in the executive office in the completed wing.

A sophisticated boat shaped cherry wood table occupied the middle of the room. It was outfitted with a built in wire management panel and a control panel to operate the television, phone system, and computer. It was state of the art. Ten high back black leather chairs surrounded the table. The view overlooked the city. The skyline of Carson City was magnificent.

"What is this and when did it happen?" Olivia asked.

"Well now that the cat is out the bag. This is new home of GT Enterprises. I was waiting to surprise you all. I know things have been a bit rocky here and in your own lives but this is who I am. But if you decided to continue to roll with me your offices would be somewhere out there." She pointed towards the outside. "But that's not why we are here."

"This is really nice. And expensive." Tressa added. "You are really serious about taking this to the next level."

"Yeah, I figured I would compartmentalize what I do and have a separate entity just for missing children. But we will see." The events of the day had her reconsidering the life she had been built around GT Investigations. The price was too much to pay.

"Ladies, we can do all the oohing and ahhing later about the new digs which I agree are quite nice. The finished product is going to be nothing short of amazing by the looks of it." Marissa carried on as though this was new to her as well but she'd been privy to a front row seat of everything. "Ok, Gay what's up."

"Let's see where do I begin? Ummmm I think somebody is on to us." She cut to the chase. "They sent Bob. Bob is probably the caller."

"Wait a minute. I thought the calls had stopped?" Tressa asked dumbfounded. "I got like two or three a few months back but nothing to the point that made me think someone was trying to intimidate me."

"Me too." Olivia concurred. "I think I got a few in the same week shortly after Bob showed up and maybe 1 or 2 last week. Didn't think much of it maybe a bad connection or a wrong number. Then again I don't hold the phone long enough to see if it's a prank. I give it about two hellos and then I hang up."

"Well I think Marissa and I have been getting the calls. Today the person finally said something.'

"And?" Olivia stood and leaned on the desk. Unnerved by the new information she was unable to sit down.

"The caller said his client wasn't happy with me investigating him and he wanted me to stop in addition to turning over all the evidence I had collected." She paused to eject the screen from the ceiling. "Did you all bring the files you had with you?"

"Yeah." The ladies simultaneously reached in their bags to retrieve them.

"What else did he say? It was a he right?"

"Yeah. It was a male. He wanted the files turned over and other files destroyed. Being the bad ass that I am I ruffled his feathers. Then he pulled the Ace of spades on me and blew my hand out the water."

"Huh?" Olivia was confused.

"He pulled the ace and mentioned Naja."

"What? So he knows you have a daughter? Does he know where you live?"

"I suspect if he knows that much he knows quite a bit more. He's smart." Gay nodded. "Very smart. As he put it it's rare that the hunter is hunted."

Tressa had been quiet and listening. "Damn. That's cold."

"So what are we going to do?"

"We?" Tressa asked with extreme concern. "I told y'all. Just give the man what he wants. Call the cops or something. But don't play this cat and mouse shit."

"Calm down Tressa! Damn! Hear her out first. You keep asking all these questions and providing your own answers. Now is not the time." Marissa added her two cents.

"I'm just saying."

"Saying what Tressa? We know how you feel. We've heard you a hundred times. You keep showing up so either you are in or you're out." The tension in the room was thickening.

"It's alright. It's my mess and I will fix it." Gay wanted to go along to get along. "I just need to go through the files and try to narrow down who the client is. The caller said he was wealthy and well known."

"That leaves nobody but Mr. Parker Monroe. Unless you got something else going on that we don't know about." Olivia asked with uncertainty.

Gay pulled up her electronic records and plugged in the photos on the screen. The software was similar to a PowerPoint program but was interactive. "Nothing else is going on with me but it looks like something is up with Mr. Monroe. There is something he does not want me -- us to know and it looks like he will go to great lengths in keeping this from us." This revelation only piqued Gay's curiosity and secretly Marissa's as well.

"I'm not going to hold you long. I know everybody has to get to work in the morning. Let's go around the room quickly and tell me what you got on Mr. CEO even if you think we already know."

Tressa went first. "Mr. CEO is married and has been having an affair with the Mayor of Las Vegas, Mrs. Kimberly LaSalle. The affair has been going for three years now. His wife discovered the affair from a hotel receipt and hired you- Gay to get concrete evidence. She's planning to divorce him and take as much of his assets as she can after discovering the affair was still going on after she confronted him and he promised to end it."

"Alrighty then. Tressa thank you for that long biographical context."

"You're welcome." A roll of her eyes confirmed her feelings of being over it.

"What do you have Olivia?"

"He is the CEO and founder of Parker Development that has interests in real estate development, banking and securities. On paper that is. He launders money from illegal gambling and prostitution into these quote-unquote, on paper, interests. Looks like that's his biggest connection to Vegas besides the lady in waiting."

"How long has he been doing the other and when did you all find that out?" This was new to Gay. She had wrapped her investigation and given everything to Mrs. Monroe, received the final check with a hefty 20% bonus and made the deposit.

"Marissa?" Olivia turned the question to her.

"Well, I've kinda been doing a little research on my own."

"What's kinda and why? Indulge me."

"I guess curiosity got the best of me. I've had dinner with this man and his wife on numerous occasions. He was just too polished and I knew there was more. Then, the meeting at the hotel. When you told me about the odd couple that met with them. I just wanted to know more."

"But you do see how this probing has possibly put me and Naja in danger. All roads lead to me not you. Not us but me. What else? How is Mrs. LaSalle connected?"

"It's obvious. Without sin city there would be no action." Olivia interjected. "Kimberly is the gate keeper to making all the transactions happen. Exactly how she is doing it is yet to be seen."

Gay pulled her locs in deep thought, tuning the ladies in and out as she processed everything that they were saying. The meeting with them, the two men, seemed strange but insignificant to her and the reason why she was to follow him to LA. Having told his wife he was attending conference that never occurred was the material fact, coupled with Mrs. LaSalle joining him.

Marissa snapped her fingers towards Gay to get her attention. "Are you following?"

"I'm following. Still not sure why you took upon on yourself to keep digging. Even if you two were working, dining, developing... All those would be reasons why I would distance myself. That's a little too close for comfort I would think."

"Point taken. But now that we are here, what do we do with it all," Gay waved her hand over the files in a circular motion. "All this evidence?"

"This is your show boss. You tell me. But I need to know quickly and as close as this caller is; I suspect that it won't be long before he's paying you a visit. Maybe Jonathan. Then the rest of us."

Sitting back down Marissa looked stunned. She had not thought that far to the extent of how much more digging she would do and what exactly she planned to do with the information she found. "Ok Gay I hear you. I'm done. Well almost."

"What does that mean?" All the while Olivia and Tressa just watched turning their heads from time to time to look at the person speaking. "What does almost mean?"

"There is a convention coming in and they are working to bring in at least 100 girls. Mr. Risner also has some real slick and dirty shit going on but his girls are younger."

"His girls? What do you mean younger. Stop talking in riddles."

Tressa responded this time. "What she means is he's involved with buying and selling younger girls across the border."

"Human trafficking?" Gay sat up, straight mind-blown.

"It looks like it. So, not trying to speak for Marissa, but I think this is the point of contention. Mr. Monroe is liaising with a man who not only prostitutes women but children as well."

"Prostituting women is a pretty hard sell. This is not the 60's and we are talking about Vegas. Brothels are legal here."

"Yeah, they are, but when you don't have an organized establishment because you are trying to avoid paying taxes, doctors, insurance and what ever else, then..."

"Then that's between them and the IRS and the Feds."

"Well, they are already on it."

"So what's the deal? It won't be long before they swoop in." Gay still wasn't getting the answers she wanted. It wasn't making sense."

"That wasn't much of the concern. The children are." Tressa showed support for Marissa.

"You say children. I thought it was girls?"

"Mostly but if someone wants a boy Mr. Risner and Norwood delivers. It looks like there's a quasi safe house just outside of Tijuana."

"Hold up! You aren't serious right now?" She didn't ask out of disbelief but more like sign me up.

"Interested now?" Marissa asked.

"A tad." Gay wasn't going to let on that she wanted a piece of this action. That was the premise of GT Enterprises and the reason to get the office. To find these children and bring them home. They were getting into something very deep. And from all appearances Marissa and Tressa had done an extensive amount of legwork on their own dime and time. They were going for the jugular and Gay wanted to ensure they had all the grip they needed. Especially with the fire Parker Monroe decided to play with. She was going to burn his ass and burn him good. Walking to the window and looking down over the city. She pulled her dreads around either side of her face and nodded. "Yeah I'm interested."

The monitor read 2:30am. "We gotta get out of here y'all." Olivia signaled she was ready to go. Having been the quietest all night she didn't want to do the whole back and forth. She would take what she knew home with her and figure out her next move on her own. Maybe it was time to let Cato in. She had been seeing him for some time now but deliberately kept the side action away from him.

"Gay Thibodeaux." She held up her finger as to say give her a minute to the ladies. The caller ID displayed a number she didn't recognize. "Gay Thibodeaux." She answered again.

"Burning the midnight oil are we?" The gruffly voice from earlier spoke.

"Isn't it past your bedtime?" She put the phone on speaker.

"Shouldn't you be home with Naja? It's definitely past her bedtime."

"Go to hell. I'm on to you."

The caller laughed. "Now you and I both know that is not true. But go ahead and psyche yourself."

"Watch me!" She screamed into the phone. "I'm going to be on your ass like white on rice."

"I'm watching my dear. Give Olivia, Marissa, and Tressa

my love."

All the women stood up. Olivia stepped out in the hall to look around the others rushed to the window. The caller's voice was rough but stalker like. He spoke calm and slow. Gay slammed the phone down. She made a mental note to put a call in to Mike and John when the sun came up.

"Excuse me ladies." They all jumped at the voice. "Didn't mean to frighten you. I'm just doing my rounds and noticed some movement behind the paper. Shadows. I thought you were gone by now."

"Oh no. Thanks for stopping by. We're getting ready to leave now and if you don't mind we could use an escort to the garage."

"Sure let me radio down and let my partner know. Ready when you are."

"If you all have time let's get together like tomorrow." Shrugging her shoulders Gay asked.

"We'll see." Tressa responded while Olivia walked towards the elevator saying nothing.

Pulling into the driveway Gay pulled the gun out the holster and laid it on her lap. "Thanks Rissa for taking care of Naja."

"Damn, It's serious right now?" Marissa looked at the gun Gay's lap then up at her.

"Pretty much."

"Stay here tonight."

"I'm good. Get in there and get some rest. Jonathan's waiting on you." Gay pointed to the house. Jonathan was sure enough standing in the window looking out.

GETTING AN UNDERSTANDING

Cato came bearing gifts. "Hello beautiful." Handing Olivia a bouquet of fresh orange Lilies, blue Iris, and pink and yellow fresh-cut Dutch Tulips, he leaned in for a kiss. Before accepting the flowers, Olivia grabbed his cleaned shaven face into her hands and kissed him slowly and deeply.

"Thank you. They are gorgeous and so fragrant."

"I should bring flowers more often." Cato smiled. "What was that for?"

"Just because."

"Because you deserve it."

Olivia was very emotional and fragile. Having pushed the last 5 clients until the next day, she decided to go home and rest while waiting for Cato to get off of work. Cato was a banker and held banker's hours. She set the alarm to get up at 5 to shower and tidy her bedroom. She had left instructions for the housekeeper to not disturb her and do everything but the vacuuming. She would handle that.

Having recently settled her newly built ranch style home, it still smelled of new carpet and paint. She was hardly home to enjoy it these days. She couldn't help but smile when she thought about how she had accomplished this on her own as a hair stylist. Foregoing the option to use her degree in education, Olivia decided against a business loan and was confident in making her plan work. Starting out in a local salon, she lived modestly because her goal was to open her own salon in two years, max. Jackpot winnings from a crazy weekend in Vegas cut the two years in half. With the success of the business and leftover winnings she decided to step out on faith and do what she dreamed of, much like Gay. There were no children or student loans, so the next thing was home ownership.

"I'll take it. Are you hungry baby? I brought groceries."

"I can eat." Olivia flashed a smile. She was happy to have him there. "What did you get?"

"I felt like Italian. So how about herb-roasted chicken, mushrooms, caramelized onions & marsala cream sauce over rigatoni?"

"Sounds delicious. What do you need me to do?"

"Grab the pots and pan. I may have you do some little slicing and dicing. And a glass of wine would be nice."

"How about wine and a little music to get the party started off right."

"It's your party baby. So you can have whatever you like." Cato accommodated.

The kitchen was getting more use these days. Cato had paid his way through college working as a sous chef in some of the finest restaurants in Dallas. He loved cooking for others, but his heart was in banking and helping people to become financially stable. Olivia afforded him the chance to marry the two as often as possible. He would prepare a great meal and they would talk money over meals.

"How was your day?" Olivia asked while taking a sip of Pinot Noir.

"I can't complain. A lot of meetings, number crunching, and talking. But all in all good. How about you?"

"You want the feel good answer or the real answer?"

"I want whatever you feel like giving me. Remember this is a judgment free zone baby. Come on lay them burdens down. Big daddy got you." Cato stopped chopping the parsley, looked at Olivia and gave her his undivided attention.

"Where have you been all....all my life?"

"Waiting on you to stop giving those knuckleheads the time of day." He laughed.

"Hey. Hey. That sounds like judging mister." She punched him softly in the shoulder.

"Ouch! That was a mean punch, and yep I did judge a little. But that was then. This." He pointed at her and then himself. "This is now."

"True."

"Now, you were saying, about your day."

"Yeah, about that. I had a long night helping Gay and Olivia with some things. Was absolutely wore out. Still a bit wore out. Cancelled all my evening clients. Gonna have to make it up to them." Half speaking and thinking she rambled. "But you're here now so it's all better."

"Poor baby. I'm sorry to hear your day has been crappy."

"You always know what to say."

"You make it easy.."

"Shhh. Hold that thought." Olivia put her finger to his lips, took a long sip of wine and grabbed his hand pulling him to the other side of the kitchen island. "You hear that?"

"A little. Turn it up."

"Oops, there goes my shirt up over my head. Oh my Oops, there goes my skirt droppin' to my feet." Olivia sang along with Tweet while she dutty wined. Starting with her head, her body was soon in full motion. Holding Cato's hand with her free one, she moved slowly to the beat being careful to accentuate the movement her hips. Slowly and seductively she dance around him and he followed. The simmering of marsala and chicken filled the room. Everything about that moment was perfect.

They decided to have dinner in the sunroom that stepped down just off of the kitchen. The weather was perfect. A few open windows allowed the evening breeze to blow through. Olivia set the table, using her bouquet of flowers as the centerpiece. A few candles gave it just the touch of elegance it needed.

"Thank you Father for this evening of food and fellowship for we know without you none of this is possible. Thank you for Olivia. Continue to grow her, prosper her, comfort her and give her peace concerning what troubles her. Amen."

Tears poured down Olivia's face. Cato's blessing of the food was more than a simple prayer but he asked for something for Olivia that she didn't ask for.

"It's ok." He walked around and put his arms around her to comfort her. "It's ok. It's already done. You don't have to say a word. But you do have to eat. A brother worked hard." Cato laughed. Whatever was going on, he didn't want Olivia to feel pressured to talk knowing that if she wanted to she would on her own time.

"I needed that."

"That's why I'm here."

"I needed that laugh and the prayer."

"It's all good."

Olivia admired Cato for so many reasons. He was a great father. He was a peacekeeper. While she fretted the ex-wife, he worked hard at making them both feel comfortable with one another. They had both moved on with their lives so there was no need to make each other miserable. The health and well being of his kids was his priority so whatever it took to keep that in tact would happen. He was a keeper.

"Well, since we are here, I do want to share with you what's been going on."

"Ok. Judgment free zone."

"I know you hear me talk a lot about Gay, Marissa, and Tressa..." Olivia shared everything. She left it all at the dinner table. Cato didn't ask any questions. He just listened, nodded, and refilled the glasses with wine as needed. Before the night was over, they had gone through three bottles of wine and Olivia had purged herself through words and tears.

"That's heavy. Damn. That...is...heavy." Cato paused between the words and didn't offer much more than that.

"I guess you want out now?"

"I'm not the one who sounds like I want out." Cato turned the mirror around figuratively.

"You're right." Olivia conceded.

"I will say this. You all aren't playing with amateurs here. It does sound like you are in over your head. You do have to keep your safety in mind. It's not about loyalty to your friends at this point."

"You make sense."

"I thought this kind of stuff only happened in the movies." He laughed, not in a funny way, but in an unbelievable way. "I'm tripping."

"You make sense." Olivia hung on his last words.

"I will say this and then I think we should call it a night. I can't jeopardize the safety of my boys. So as much as I want to support you on this I just may have to lay low until you all get this sorted out. I'm not sure what that means or what it looks like for you." It hurt to hear himself say that. He loved Olivia.

"I respect that."

"Let me help you to the bed and then I'll let myself out."

"What about the dishes?"

"You're something else." He laughed. "Even three bottles of wine won't let you leave a dirty kitchen."

"Nope."

"I will take care of it. Come on sweet Olivia." Helping her

to her feet he led her to the bedroom.

"Lay with me a while." Patting the side of the bed she invited him over.

Cato lay behind her and slowly rubbed her back. She moaned under his touch until she fell asleep.

JUSTICE NOT DENIED

Every person entering the courtroom for the family was given a green ribbon in solidarity for the missing children around the world. The day in court was fighting on their behalf as well. They were also given a pink rose that was symbolic for love and appreciation. There had been an outpouring of kindness from around the world after Dynasty had been found. Several stories ran across the news in both print and television. What made the story so heart wrenching was the fact that the crime had been committed against her by her peers. So many people tried wrapping their minds around how such a horrific act could happen to a someone who didn't do anything to warrant it. However, this seemed to be the sign of the times. Things were happening everyday to people who that didn't warrant it. The judge restricted the family from wearing buttons and shirts bearing Dynasty's likeness for fear of influencing the jury. Seeing a picture of the innocent teen could possibly illicit sympathy that would bias them.

Bringing the case to trial took almost a year. Many thought that it was rushed. They had not seen all the work that was going on in the background. Chief Buckner was true to his word in being relentless in leaving no stone unturned, no witness unquestioned, and no piece of evidence untested. He had been grieved by the case and had stated that he would resign his position after the trial. Having clocked enough hours to retire a few years back. It was time. This was probably the biggest thing that happened in his tenure but one of the worse things he would probably be remembered for. Probably one of the worse things the town of Merriweather County would be remembered for.

"Ready?" Tressa asked the other ladies as they sat in the car getting ready for the drive over. The Hawks had their calendar marked for the first day of the start of the trial and had made a decision to be there throughout no matter how long it took.

"I don't know if it's ever possible to be ready for something like this." Gay sighed.

The trial's venue had been changed at the request of the defense attorney. Sumner County wasn't very far however it was far enough away that the defense believed that the young men accused of the crime would get a fair trial. They did not live and work with Doris Langston who was well liked and respected in the community. She had delivered many of the babies Dynasty attended school with. She worshipped with the parents, cheered alongside them at the games, and chatted at community functions.

"Are you seeing what I'm seeing?" Olivia asked pointing at the row of media vans lined on the side of the highway leading to the courthouse. There was a small crowd on the outside and a line still waiting to get in.

"Yeah we see and it's a shame. Anything to spin a story." Marissa wasn't impressed and she was not in the mood to fight. But a letter to press associations was long overdue on how the media is used or not used. If the media was truly for the best interest of the public that mission was not being accomplished.

"Silence. All rise please. This court is now in session. The Honorable Judge Manchester presiding. You may now be seated." The bailiff instructed those attendance. The Langston family and supporters sat to the right of the judge. Doris sat on the front row and asked that the Hawks sit with her.

The three accusers would be tried together and were all charged with murder, kidnapping, sexual assault and a host of other charges. First or second-degree murder was not an option in South Carolina. The charge of murder carried a sentence of death, life without parole, 30 years to Life or 30 years in prison. All the teens had reached the age of majority to be tried as an adult except one. Prosecution pushed hard to have the lone 16 year old charged as adult and won. There were no winners in this situation.

"Your Honor, Judge Manchester, DAs Phillips and Washington and to my colleagues seated here today, good morning. Good morning to the family of Dynasty Langston. To Ms. Langston and all who support her, the real parties of interest in this case. Ladies and gentlemen good morning." The prosecutor began his opening remarks. "I first want to say we appreciate you being on the panel." Turning to the jurors and acknowledging them one by one with a nod he continued to speak. "I don't take this lightly and understand this may be the hardest job any of you have had to do. Keep in mind we are here for a central focus and that focus is to exact justice. Justice for Dynasty Langston, a young, 16 year old African American girl who had her entire life ahead of her. A life that was abruptly snatched from her and all who loved her, leaving behind a mother who lived and breathed for her daughter searching for air and a reason to continue to live and breathe."

The twelve men and women who comprised the jury sat tall and looked straight ahead occasionally turning to look around the courtroom at those in attendance as well as the defendants. Five men and 7 women was the final makeup with only three whites.

"What we have here is an indictment of murder. The indictment sets forth that Aaron Johnson, Jevontae McGruder, and Michael Wilson on the 27th of April 2000 did administer a mind-altering drug to Dynasty Langston by spiking her punch. After spiking the punch lured her into a car where they intended to have a good time with her. That good time was sex. She was chosen because she wasn't like the rest of the girls. Smart, outgoing, pretty and "didn't have time for these boys" as she was often heard saying; they were going to show her." The prosecutor painted a picture of good versus bad. "Dynasty couldn't put up much a fight at the time. After taking turns of brutally sexually assaulting her they decided they weren't done. They wanted more. Days of torture followed. Having kept her locked in a basement she met her fate when the hands of Jevontae McGruder choked the life out of her while trying to break free and escape to safety."

Until now the details of how she died were unknown. Talk around time and leaks from the investigation revealed that a drug was given to several girls, Dynasty had left with some boys and that she was probably raped. Other rumors spurred that she had been secretly dating and having sex with Aaron, that she was shot and killed and so much more. The family of the accused spoke negatively about her to the media and proclaimed the innocence of the accused, even to the extent of pointing blame at a few who could have not been remotely involved.

Pacing back and forth in front of the jury box the Prosecutor brought it all home. He needed to put the nail in the coffin. "To this charge. The charge of murder all these defendants." Walking over to the defense table pointing one by one" Aaron, Jevontae, Michael; all have pleaded not guilty. If we prove him guilty, you must find them guilty also. And we will do this. The facts are simple Aaron being friends with them invited them to the dance in which he knew they could not attend so they settled on having their own party afterwards. Aaron wasn't the mastermind but one of the minds put together to carry out the plan. He picked the girls; the other young men brought the car, and the secret weapon. Without any warning or provocation the accused came in like a thief in the night and stole something that didn't belong to them. Not only sex but also a life. In the most horrendous manner to sexually assault a young virgin time and time again for hours on end. The only crime that Dynasty committed, if you want to call it a crime, was following her mother's instruction to wait on her and not get in the car with anyone. The crime, if you want to call it a crime, was take a cup of punch from Aaron to quench her thirst."

The jurors looked towards Ms. Langston who could be seen wiping tears from her eyes. Gay sat beside her with her arm around her rubbing her shoulders.

"Bravo, bravo!" Defense Attorney Pritchard stood clapping his hands. "Good morning, Your Honor, Judge Manchester, family, friends, and ladies and gentlemen of the jury. That was quite compelling, I have to admit, but I'm not here to give you compelling. I am here to give you the facts. He painted a picture of my clients being reckless, thugs, being callous and cold-blooded murders. But what's a picture without facts. I'm going to give you facts." His voice was loud and emphatic. "He has explained that the my clients supposedly had drugged many students but failed to mention that no one else tested positive for this drug nor had any drugs or vials been found. He explained that she was lured in the car but failed to mention that plans had been made before the dance for Aaron and Dynasty to see each other afterwards. He stated that Dynasty was kept against her will for days when in fact she was too afraid and ashamed to go home. She was not the good girl purported to be. And lastly he stated that she died at the hands of one of my clients. There was somebody else there and the fact remains that she was alive when they all saw her."

There were gasps from the courtroom. The defense countered everything the prosecutor highlighted. The expressionless jurors

When No One Came

looked at the prosecutor as though they were searching for answers.

"Yes this case is tragic case. Very tragic and yes we feel for the mother. It's only natural to, but keep in mind that we have 3 lives hanging in the balance for a crime they did not commit. We ask that you stay here." He made an eye-to-eye motion. "All we're asking is that you would keep an open mind and listen to all the evidence, and return a verdict of "not guilty". They may be guilty of being rambunctious teens but murderers, they are not. Thank you."

The sound from the stenotype filled the room coupled with occasional body movement. The air was still and stale. Chief Buckner sat in the back and the room and observed what was taking place. The room was filled from corner to corner mostly from curious onlookers.

Pagers began to go off and commotion could be heard outside in the halls. "All rise. Court is adjourned for the remainder of the day and will resume at 8 in the morning. You may be seated after the Honorable Judge Manchester leaves the room. Remain seated until the defendants have been escorted out. Then you are dismissed. Please remain quiet."

***

The street and the lawns were bustling with action. Every reporter was on camera reporting. Many had convened at one of the two local diners while others stood on the corners and sidewalks talking. The abrupt ending of court was being played out on the diner's television and could be heard over the police scanners.

A ribbon of all-caps text along the bottom third at 10:49 am highlighted what everyone had soon found out. A plane had been flown directly into the North followed by the South towers of the World Trade Center in New York City. Gay scrambled for her phone. New York was home and her family was there. "**Marissa** call Deb. Tressa call Bo." She delegated as she worked through her own calls. What was understood didn't have to be explained. The ladies went to work helping her try to reach the most immediate family first. The lines were busy. No one could get through. "What the hell is going on." Gay asked in frustration not expecting an answer.

Both towers had collapsed by this time and the news channels broadcast short clips of video footage in loops of the towers collapsing. Everyone was transfixed by the terror that was unfolding. Soon after the news reported conflicting stories that more planes were hijacked and missing heightening the fear that America was under attack.

"Keep trying!" Gay's voice was less reserved this time. An hour had passed and the lines were still busy. People could be seen running down the streets of Manhattan away from the towers with the devastation in the form of ash and soot following them. T-shirts, scarves, and jackets were held to their faces to prevent inhaling the smoke. Some were bleeding about the head and face. Others were being semi-carried. The visibility was low. The media covered every angle of what was occurring. A plane had crashed into the Pentagon and another in Pennsylvania.

Gay was broken and vulnerable. The only other time since knowing Gay that the ladies had seen this was when her grandmother passed. She sat on the end of the booth dialing and hanging up the phone going down the list starting with her parents hoping she would get someone. The majority of the family lived in Brooklyn but there were several who worked in Lower Manhattan. "This can't be real. Tell me this is not happening?" Directing her questions at no one in particular.

"It's going to be alright. I'm sure there is just an overload on the phone lines right now with everyone doing the same thing we are. Trying to find out what is happening." Tressa rationed.

"Yes, I'm sure everyone is fine. Do you want something to eat?" Marissa agreed and hoped that eating would temporarily distract their minds.

"I'm not hungry." Gay responded staring out the window. "Let me go get some air. Keep trying please."

"Sure. We whatever you need." Seeing their friend, their sister lost and confused left them feeling the same. One tragic event turned into a series of tragic events. Tressa knew that this was the last straw. The emotional toll was beginning to be too much.

The ladies watched Gay from inside the restaurant. Throngs of people covered the sidewalk at this point. She could be seen weaving in and out of them working her phone.

"May I join you?" The ladies looked up to see Ms. Langston.

"Yes, please." Olivia scooted over to make room. "You can sit here." She patted the empty space beside her. "How are you?" For that moment she put their drama aside and directed her concern to Doris.

"I guess I'm alright compared to what's going on. We are in our last days. So much killing and violence going on."

"I believe." Melissa nodded while continuing to watch Gay.

"What's going on with Gay?" Ms. Langston noticed her frantically dialing her phone and pushing her locks up over her head.

Marissa and Olivia began to speak at the same time. "She has… Oops go for Olivia." Marissa pointed.

"Ms. Langston, Gay is from New York she's unable to reach her family there to see if everyone is safe."

"Irony?"

Turning to look at each at the same time, that notion had not struck them but it made perfect sense. Ms. Langston was spot on. If Gay never knew how it felt to not know the whereabouts or condition a loved one was in this was her lesson on how it felt to be helpless and hopeless.

Additional irony was the barrage of media and how quickly they shifted gears. The morning started out being all about Dynasty Langston, her murder, and the trials. At 5:34 pm it seemed as if they had forgotten about her.

***

The phone lines were still down. Gay received an email at approximately 4 in the morning from her mom confirming that everybody was ok but quite upset. Her aunt had a doctor's appointment in Brooklyn that caused her to miss work by the grace of God. She would continue to try and call but couldn't promise anything because the phone lines were out from Brooklyn to Manhattan.

Gay's eyes told a story of a tired woman. Running on two hours of sleep the ladies encouraged her to stay at the hotel and come to court after lunch but she refused.

"I'm okay."

"You don't look like it."

"Tressa, leave it to you to tell it like it is. Or as my Me-Me use to say t-i-is." She conjured up a smile.

"You're so silly."

"I would call it delirious right about now."

The scene was quite different this morning. The row of news van that had lined the street the day before were gone along with the reporters on the lawn. A handful of junior reporters and photographers were left behind. What was important to the people now was the safety of America.

"All rise...." The bailiff opened court per usual. The beauty of the historic courtroom went unnoticed by the overcrowding the day before. The raised flooring, theater-style seating and massive marble columns were immaculate. Much of the architecture remained the same from the early 1900s however the furniture was updated. Velvet window coverings hung to the floor. The color of the arched ceilings matched the floor. "Court is now in session."

"Prosecution, you may call your first witness." Judge Manchester instructed.

District Attorney Phillips stood with a note pad. "Thank you, your Honor. I call to the stand Macy Smith."

"Go on. Tell the truth. Take your time and speak loud" Macy's mom could be heard coaching her daughter before she walked to the witness stand.

Dressed in black slacks with a black and white jacket Macy walked quickly to the witness stand.

"Will the witness please stand to be sworn in by the bailiff?"

Macy stood and raised her right hand. "Do you swear to tell the truth, the whole truth, and nothing but the truth?"

Cutting her eyes to the defendants then to Ms. Langston she answered. "I do."

"Thank you for being brave Macy and thank you for being honest."

"Yes sir."

"Give us a little insight on what happened the night of the dance. What happened after you made it to the school?

"When we got there."

"I need you to be specific for the jury. Who is we?"

"When me, Dynasty, Toya, and Sheila made it to the school. We started talking to our classmates, laughing and joking around."

"Did you all stay together the entire time?"

"No, Sheila and Toya had to leave an hour early because their mom doesn't have a car, so they were getting a ride from their neighbor."

"Before they left did you all stay together the entire time?"

"No, Sheila went outside a few times to talk to some boys from Overton."

"Who are the boys from Overton? Are they in the room?"

"Yes."

"Will you point to them for the jurors?"

"They are sitting beside Aaron- Jevontae and Michael."

DA Philips jotted on his notepad. "Your honor and the jury let it be known for the record that Macy Smith has identified and placed the two defendants on the school grounds the night of the dance."

"Acknowledged." Judge Manchester agreed.

"Macy do you know what Sheila was doing when she went outside?"

"Not really? She said she was just talking and she liked Jevontae."

"Objection your honor. That's hear say." The defense stood.

"Sustained."

"Ok Macy. Did you or Dynasty ever go outside to speak with the young men seated over there?"

Looking down Macy paused before answering. "Yes."

"Please speak louder."

"Yes."

"Yes you went outside or you and Dynasty both went outside to speak with the young men sitting at that table?"

"We both went out." Her voice was barely audible.

"Why did you do that?"

"We liked them and wanted to talk to them. Aaron kept asking."

The line of questioning went back and forth. Witness after witness. All in all over 10 students and 3 adults were called. The adults were the apart of the group that chaperoned the dance with one testifying that she had last seen Dynasty talking to Aaron near the car with the two other defendants. She turned to help another student only to see the car and Dynasty gone. The sticking point with this witness and the credibility in the story rested in the fact that she was visiting the area at the time and no one was able to track her afterwards.

The defense went back and forth about allowing Aaron testify. He was a minor being charged as an adult, and to the objection of the defense, his mom insisted that he be allowed on the witness stand, which proved to be detrimental. Aaron nailed his own coffin shut.

"Aaron when was the last time you saw or spoke to Dynasty Langston?"

"The night of the dance. When it was over I asked her if she was going to finally give me her number. She said no. I said cool and left with my friends."

"When you say your friends who are they?"

"Jevontae and Michael."

"Why were they at the school? They didn't attend the school?" DA Phillips asked.

"They came to pick me up. I was going to spend the weekend in Overton with them."

"Are you saying they were not there prior to the dance being over? Take your time and think about your response."

When No One Came

"Uhhhh they weren't there too long."

"Are you sure that is the last time you saw Dynasty? We have other witnesses who say otherwise. You heard them say otherwise."

Aaron looked out and locked eyes with Ms. Langston who was staring him in the face. He quickly turned his head. The DA asked again. "Are you sure that is the last time you saw Dynasty?"

"Mr. Pritchard. I need to talk to you." Aaron avoided the question and called on his attorney.

"Your Honor instruct the witness to answer the question."

"Mr. Pritchard I can't do this." Aaron continued to speak to his attorney while ignoring the prosecutor."

"Order! Order in the court." Judge Manchester banged the gavel down. By this time the few people inside could be heard mumbling. "Mr. Pritchard would you like to call a recess to speak with your client?" Baffled Judge Manchester asked.

"Yes, Your Honor. I would like to request a 15 minute recess to speak with my client."

Confusion filled the courtroom. "What's happening? What? What's going on" were all questions that filled the air. The bailiff asked for continued order as the judge left for his chambers.

"Maybe this is the break we've been praying for." Gay spoke to Ms. Langston. She had been praying that somebody would confess and save everyone the details and agony that came along with murder trials. The fifteen minutes seemed like eternity but within that short time frame and a meeting within chambers between the prosecutor and the defense the tides had changed.

"Your Honor we would like to enter a motion to change our plea from guilty to not guilty."

Instead of a thunderous applause or shouts of victory the room was shocked into quiet. Doris Langston wept quietly. Not knowing rather to be happy or sad she wept quietly. She was sad for the young men who also had their entire lives ahead of them who would spend the rest of it behind bars. She was sad for the parents who now would grieve the loss of their children. She was just sad. And a tiny bit of her soul was glad knowing that Dynasty was heaven with her dad.

While there were still so many questions about what could have been done different Chief Buckner had his day. He tilted his had towards the ladies and left the courtroom without saying anything to anyone.

TOO CLOSE FOR COMFORT

"Hello beautiful." Olivia kissed Marissa on the cheek as they embraced.

"Hello beautiful yourself. Let me look at you." She stepped back while holding onto Marissa and gave her the once over. "How have you been?"

"You know I can't complain. Work, Jonathan, work. You know the routine."

"Do I?" She laughed. "Work, the boo, work, the boo."

"So the boo has survived?"

"Yes, his ex-wife turned out to be sane after all." Olivia giggled. "Let me stop. He is about business when it comes to his family. I think mature people can always find a way to make it work."

"Good for you. You deserve all the happiness you can stand."

"You think so?"

"I know so."

"It wont be any to stand if I don't let this go."

"Why you say that?"

"Cato supports me but doesn't want his or the boys' safety be compromised because someone is not ok with me. We've talked about it and I overstand where he's coming from. Hell, I don't want my own safety compromised."

"Yeah, I think we at the crossroads. Jonathan is more than a ready for a baby. I promised a year and it's been more than that."

The days rolled into weeks and the weeks rolled into months. The ladies had been laying low contemplating their next moves. The phone calls continued to come in but they were less frequent. The Langston case caused them to take a step back and really evaluate if that was a space they wanted to be in. The time, effort and commitment needed to effectively assist a family in locating loved ones required more than they had. A full time staff was needed to take care of the administrative side of things, at least five full-time, highly skilled investigators, equipment, and connections to people and resources that went far up the chain and as low into the crime world were critically needed. This was something they knew at first, but Gay underestimated the seriousness of it all. They were committed to at least trying. Gay had made it up in her mind that she would be in for the long haul.

"I'm glad we finally found time in our busy schedules to sit and down and genuinely connect." Marissa smiled. "And as usual half of this quad is late."

Smiling back Olivia added. "It wouldn't be right if everyone was on time. I'm glad as well, but I do suspect that there has been some avoidance and stalling. We live in the same city, not more than 15-20 minutes--max, from each other. So, between Christmas and now, no time to relax, relate, release? Ummmm you tell me. And business meetings don't count. They are always stuffy and serious."

"I agree. I think it's just been a lot to wrap our minds around."

As with most things, not until it's in your own backyard does a person have the ability to connect with real life issues. "I have to be honest, in my mind I just thought it would be something as simple as making a few phone calls and asking a few questions and the parents would be somewhat satisfied." Olivia confided.

"Yeah I think we all did."

The Blue Lagoon was bustling with business. Patrons moved in and out the patio. The smell of sizzling fajitas and other Mexican fare filled the air with the sound of laughter and hearty conversation. "Excuse me Senoritas, please accept these margaritas courtesy of the gentleman over there." The waiter turned to point at an empty chair near the patio bar. "He's no longer there."

The ladies looked in the direction the waiter was pointing. "Who, the dark haired gentleman?" Marissa asked.

"He's not there anymore, but he ordered these drinks and asked me to deliver to you two."

"Can you describe him?"

"I don't want any trouble."

"No trouble. We're just curious to know who the nice gentleman was. Our friends are always playing jokes on us."

"I've never seen him before. But that doesn't mean that he hasn't come when I wasn't working. He was an older white man, had a ball cap on, wrinkle skin, smelled like cigars."

That description fit the mysterious Bob perfectly. "Thank you. You can take these back. Olivia stay here I'm going to look around."

"Ok! Be careful."

"We are in broad daylight. I doubt he try anything stupid in front of all these people."

"Ok. Hurry back." Olivia agreed half-heartedly. "Gay! Where are y'all? Bob is here or someone near by." She quickly called Gay. "Thanks ummm. Ricardo." Reading his nametag. "Did he pay with a credit card or cash?"

"I think he paid with cash but let me check."

Olivia didn't know what Bob looked like but remembered the description Tressa and Marissa had given. Looking around she tried to see if anyone was on the patio that remotely resembled him.

"Olivia come out and look to the right. We are standing with Bob." Gay called.

At the end of the corner opposite the front door of the Blue Lagoon Olivia could see the other ladies talking to a tall white man. She contemplated joining them. They were out in broad daylight on one of the busiest streets, which guaranteed that nothing would happen. Unless Bob was a complete lunatic.

"Bob or whatever your name is. What is the damn deal?" Gay served up much attitude.

"There is no deal. It looks like some very important people are willing to pay top dollar to keep tabs on you. All of you."

"Tabs for what?" Olivia had made her way to the group. "There isn't much to being a stylist."

"Don't insult my intelligence. I know what all of you do and what you don't do. So let's quit with the games."

"I just wanted to make my presence known. Next time I just might …just might … make it felt. That's all up to you." He snarled.

Bob's voice was not the same as the one on the phone, which let the ladies know they were dealing with at least two different people who had a good visual on them.

"What do you mean?" Olivia pretended to be naïve.

"No need to play dumb. You know exactly what I'm talking about. There has been a certain request made and we are still waiting. So you can choose to do this our way or your way- the hard way."

This time Gay interjected. Standing far enough from Bob she opened her blazer revealing the gun in the holster. "Easy or hard I like it both ways. Come on ladies- better yet come on Hawks." Gay turned and spoke over her shoulders. "Tell your boss we got his number too."

Bob tipped his bib and walked off with a smirk on his face. "Damn I like her." He smiled to himself.

Gay walked back towards the Blue Lagoon stopping to tap the driver's side window of a black Yukon parked near the curb. A crack in the window showed Mike and John sitting inside. Her extra dose of courage came from her extra set of eyes and hands.

Little did the ladies know they were being tailed as well by ex-military personnel who now moonlighted as personal security guards.

"Come on slow poke. We're hungry." Marissa called to Gay.

"Go on in and order for me."

"Sure. You have 5 minutes."

"Ok, Let me talk to the fellas for a sec. Then I'll be there."

Mike rolled the window down further. "What was that about?"

"That was Bob?"

"Did he say what he wanted?"

"Why didn't you get out and ask him what he wanted?"

"Gay you know it doesn't work like that."

"Wishful thinking. Maybe if he saw you he wouldn't come back around."

"I suspect he doesn't scare that easily. Especially when hunting someone with a nice bounty on their head."

"Bounty? Do tell."

"Gay, you're a little fish trying to swim in a pond of sharks. But we got this."

"As long as you got my back. I'll take care of the front."

Mike winked and rolled up the window. Gay had not noticed the black Camaro parked on the other side of the street the entire time. It was camouflaged by two other black cars, one parked in the front of it and the other in the rear of it. What she did notice was someone exiting the passenger side and heading in her direction. It was an African American man. About 6 feet tall with a stocky build. She turned to the black Yukon and pointed. Mike and John not wanting to jump the gun waited inside and watched.

"My, my, my. Ms. Gay Thibodeaux. The Gay Thibodeaux. The Gay Thibodeaux of GT investigations."

"Who wants to know?"

"Wouldn't you like to know?" He walked and talked at the same time forcing Gay backwards onto the wall.

"You're in my space and I suggest that unless you have anything of importance to say besides introducing me to myself you continue to walk past me or turn around and walk back to your car."

The stranger stepped back and held her against the wall with one hand in her chest. The few onlookers walked by as if they didn't notice. Many probably believed this to be a domestic violence situation and didn't want to get involved.

Gay turned towards Mike and John with a distressed look on her face.

"Get your damn hands off of me."

"What's all that shit you were talking on the phone. Something about burning my ass? Well as you can see I'm already black so not much to burn. You have 48 hours to drop the info." He pushed her chest harder.

"You know I've tried to play nice." Looking up and into his eyes. "I'm going to ask you one more time to get your damn hands off of me."

"Or?"

By that time John and Mike were behind him standing on either side. "Or, say hello to my big friends."

The stranger turned to see John and Mike. No words were exchanged but he had swapped placed with Gay on the wall. "Hey buddy! Is that how you are supposed to treat a woman? Didn't your momma raise you better?" Without waiting for a response Mike landed a punch to his right side and John to the left.

"Ok fellas. I know you would like to have a little more fun but I suspect the cops may be on the way."

"We suspect you're right. We've been waiting on Mr. John Beedle aka Johnny Boy." John offered a little insight about the stranger.

"So you know him?"

"We know of him. He's an ex- cop gone rogue. Does a little rough up work here and there."

John bent over holding his face. "Watch your back."

"So are you threatening us? You know we don't take threats lightly." Mike came down on his back with a sharp elbow.

"Ok Mike! Damn you see he's all talk. I think he's had enough."

"I'm sure he has and this is the last time you'll see him?" John held the other John's chin up and nodded.

"What took you so long?"

When No One Came

"Just waiting to see how you would handle up." Mike laughed. "What took you so long?"

"That's what I'm paying you two for right?"

"Point taken." Mike laughed. "Oh Gay! You're something else."

"I've heard that before. Good job boys." She gave them a high five and headed to the restaurant to the ladies in waiting.

***

Water poured rapidly from the sky causing the streets to turn into makeshift wading pools. The weather was forecasted to be clear, sunny with a high of 85 degrees. The Hawks had been to Florida several times since the bikes were discovered --a few times as a group, and other times, two at a time. The activity ebbed and flowed around the case. After a story ran, they were inundated with calls and possible sightings, then there periods where there was nothing. Josalyn would soon be turning 14 and was still missing. The Mabreys decided to highlight the anniversary of when she was last seen with a call to action. This call to action included community mobilization involving searches, door-to-door canvassing, and new posters with an age progression image. For this trip, Gay would go alone. The other ladies were burning the candle at both ends with their regular jobs and trying to keep up with GT Investigations.

"Hello darling." Mrs. Mabrey's eyes lit up when she saw her. "I'm so glad to see you."

"I'm glad that you are glad to see me." Gay smiled and hugged her.

"Anything new?"

"I think you know just about everything. They are still waiting for the results from the crime lab. Something about running them in a database to see if they get any matches."

"That's the National Crime Information Center database. They have files on just about everything from stolen goods, guns, license plates, cars and registries for sex offenders and missing people."

Mrs. Mabrey looked surprised. "That's a lot of information. No wonder it's taking so long."

"It still shouldn't take this long. The information is organized in a particular way along with everything being electronic now they should've gotten a hit or miss within a few weeks. Don't worry I'm headed to see Detective Graham in a bit then I will head over to the park."

"I can't thank you enough."

"You already have. See you in a little while."

The police station was quiet, aside from the occasional ring of the phone and conversation from desk to desk. Many of the officers were at the park assisting with setup and community mobilizations. Each year more activities were being added. Mobile units offered free child identification kits that included photographs and finger printing along with pertinent information about physical characteristics. Everyone in attendance was encouraged to take advantage of this free service for all children 15 and under and fingerprinting for those over 15 if they had a driver's permit/license already.

"I'm here to see Detective Graham."

"Hi Gay. We were wondering if you all were going to make it down this weekend." Officer Rodgers greeted her. Having been assigned to work directly with the ladies he had become very familiar with them. He was the point of contact for all key developments.

"The other ladies didn't make this trip but I'm here. How is everything going?"

"It's going. Praying everyday that something turns up."

"That's all of us. Anything new since we last spoke?"

"We had a few possible sightings call. One as far away as Canada. You know I'm starting to think that people do think we all look alike." He shook his head.

"That bad huh?"

"That bad. I mean some of the girls I could see but others didn't remotely resemble Josalyn. Either they were blind or were hoping to cash in on the reward money."

"Not surprised. How is that going?"

"We're up to 50 thousand now."

"That's promising."

"I've seen rewards start at 50. I guess folk just donate to these like this."

"They do but…. Ummm don't get me on my soapbox. Is Detective Graham here?"

"He ran over to the print shop but should be back in a bit. I know he wanted to finish up some things before he went to the park. He figured he'd be too pooped, in his words, to come back to the office. Oh, and speaking of the reward money, we did receive two phone calls last week asking how much it was now. I thought it strange that someone called just asking about that."

"Did you get a number?

"Yeah it was one of those pre-paid accounts."

"Keep an eye on that. It's definitely strange."

"Speak of the devil." Officer Rodgers laughed. "Hey Graham!"

"I told you about that Rodgers. The devil is red and has horns. I got one of the two." He laughed wiping sweat from his forehead. "Excuse my manners. Hello Ms. Thibodeaux."

"Hi Detective Graham. Is it hot enough for you?"

"It's so hot, I saw squirrels fanning their nuts."

"Ok, didn't we just take a sexual harassment class?"

"We did and Ms. Thibodeaux isn't a part of this workforce so I'm safe."

"Hey, hey respect the lady."

Shaking her head and laughing. "I see you guys are still up to your shenanigans."

"Makes the day go by faster."

"Hold that thought; better yet don't you have work to do?" Detective Graham chided before answering his cell phone. "Detective Graham. Yes. Checking now." Speaking to the caller on the other end of the line he beckoned Gay to follow him in his office.

"What's up?" Gay didn't wait for him to clue her in.

"Logging in now. That was NCIC informing me of a hit on the bike. Actually they had two hits beside Josalyn, Tony, and Jackie."

"Rodgers, will you grab those papers off the printer for me?"

Gay paced the floor in anticipation. "You're making me nervous. It's ok to sit."

"Yeah, I know just anxious."

"Here ya go."

"Pull up a seat." Detective Graham invited Officer Rodgers to join them. "Ok, let's see what we have here." Looking at the profiles. The first was that of a 28-year-old white woman. Long, dark hair weighing approximately 120 pounds. She had an abdominal scar and a number of tattoos most notable a barbed wire extending around her neck. It was also noted that she had 4 piercing- both ears, nose, and tongue. She had been released from jail two weeks prior to Josalyn's disappearance.

"And this person's prints were found on Josalyn's bike?" Officer Rodgers asked confused.

"According to the crime lab."

Gay read the other profile. "David Moore, 52 year old African American male. Rap sheet longer than all our arms put together from petty crimes, to rape, to armed robbery. This dude has spent more than half of his life behind bars. Two hundred pounds, 5 feet 4. Scar on the right side of his cheek from his eye to his mouth. Both ears pierced and he was last in prison a year before Josalyn's disappearance."

"What were they doing together?"

"We'll figure that out once we find them. Won't we? Gay responded.

"Rodgers, go run them and make sure they aren't in anyone else's jail. With their history they just may be. See if you get a different address than what we have here."

Gay stood up again and paced the floor while reading through the profiles. "It says here that the last known address is in WinterGrade. How far is that?"

"WinterGrade is actually 20-25 minutes from here."

"So we should be headed there."

"Hold on Gay. We don't know if they're even there."

"Ok, this is what I have." Officer Rodgers ran into the room. "They are not in jail. The young lady Amanda Cobb was picked up last week for public intoxication. She spent a night in jail over in Boyd County. Looks like they are still over at WinterGrade address. When are we going?"

"Rodgers, I need you here, but get me the Sheriff over there and call at least 5 officers back to the station to go over there with me. I need a search warrant ASAP. As soon as we get that we can go."

"I'm on it."

"Rodgers I don't need you to call ANYONE else or talk about this." Detective Graham gave a stern look. "Thank you."

"I'm going to step and call the ladies about this development, then head to the park and wait for your call. How long does it usually take to get the search warrant?"

"It shouldn't take too long. This kinda thing doesn't happen all the time so there's no waiting line. Need to have that in hand so if there is anything they won't have time to dump it."

"Makes sense."

"Oh Gay, let's keep this right here for now. I don't want anybody interfering."

"I'm right here." Gay motioned from her eyes to his.

***

547 Pecan Grove was the last doublewide trailer on the right of the street. The siding was falling off one side and the yard was overgrown with grass and weeds. There wasn't much trash in the yard. Sheets were covering the windows. A tire swing hung from the lone tree in the back of the house. Detective Graham met Sheriff Tatum at the station and followed him there. A police car blocked the entrance of the street preventing traffic from entering or leaving. Two officers were instructed to go door to door on either side of the street and cautioning residents to stay inside. Two more officers were instructed to stay at the rear of the house in case someone tried to run.

"Does everyone have on their vests? Does everyone know what the people we are looking for look like?"

"We're ready." The officers responded.

"Vest- check, warrant- check, gun- check." Detective Graham did a once over. "Gay I think you should wait here for us."

"Come on Detective Graham. This case is my baby. I've come too far to be this close and have to sit in the car. Josalyn could be inside."

"Along with guns and other danger." He tried to reason.

"I know about guns. I own one. I know how to shoot one and damn well I might add." Gay wasn't backing down.

"Damn Gay! Come on but stay behind. You don't have any protection but that vest." Detective Graham gave in.

The makeshift curtain could be seen moving. "Someone has eyes on us." Sheriff Tatum spoke.

"And we do too. Let's go!" Detective Graham pointed towards door instructing everyone to move forward.

"Police! Police! Open up." Knocking on the door with extra force Detective Graham called out. "Police!"

No one answered the door. But there could be movement and rustling heard from inside. The movement of the curtain already revealed someone was inside. Detective Graham stepped to the side and nodded giving the queue for the other officer to kick the door in.

Officers could be heard asking people to get back inside to keep the streets empty.

"Get down! Get down! Don't even try it!" An officer yelled from behind the house. "We have the male suspect back here."

"We're going in." Sheriff Tatum spoke loud enough for the other officers to hear as well as anyone inside the house.

At this point there was no talking but a series of hand movements. Detective Graham was leading the efforts. The front door opened into the living room. There were rooms on either side of the trailer and a kitchen area could be seen off to the right. All the officers had their guns drawn. He tapped one officer on the shoulder and pushed him in the direction of the right followed by instructing another to the left. Detective Graham remained in the living room with Gay watching from the doorway. Sheriff Tatum had made his way to the rear of the house.

"Get your hands in the air and keep them there." The officer gave warning from the right side of the house.

"I need one more officer." Detective Graham called for more assistance. The house wasn't gigantic but it had enough rooms that they wanted to cover all bases. They knew they were dealing with a career criminal, but didn't know what else or who else. "Hold this post." Detective Graham walked over to the right side to get a better view. "Take him out."

The officer emerged from the room with a white male who had his hands up in the air. He wore blue jeans and a dirty white t-shirt. His pockets were turned inside out and he didn't have on socks or shoes. His hair was matted at the back.

"Detective Graham you need to see this!" The officer called from the left. "The bedroom to the right."

Gay followed him. It was something about how the officer said you have to see this. The trailer was not filthy but it wasn't clean either. It was simple with only a few pieces of furniture- sofa, coffee table, chair, and television. The kitchen had a table with 4 chairs, a small microwave and mismatched stove and refrigerator. The bedroom to which Detective Graham was directed had a twin bed, a small brown dresser and butterflies painted in the wall. This was the only room that had curtains. The curtains matched the blanket.

"Josalyn?" Gay called out from the door. She was spooked. The room felt like Josalyn. The butterflies, the color, the neatness. "Josalyn?" she called again.

Amanda stood in the far corner. She didn't say anything but pointed to the closet. The officer had found both of them kneeling down in the closet under a blanket.

"What the hell?" Those were the only words Detective Graham could utter.

Gay stepped around him and walked to the closet. "Are you Josalyn Mabrey?"

The girl who was no longer 10 but looked exactly the same with the exception of acne and a cropped haircut. Josalyn grabbed Gay's hand and stood up. "I am Josalyn Mabrey. I am 14 years old. Amanda and David kidnapped me when I was 10. My mother's name is Jacqueline Mabrey and my father is Tony Mabrey. My address is 3242 Millcreek Drive." She spoke robotically.

"Yes Josalyn. I know you and you are safe. We have been looking for you for a long time. Your parents Jackie and Tony have been looking for you for a long time. Today they are actually having a party just for you." Gay spoke softly and child like.

***

The park was filled with community members as well as residents from the subdivision. KRV7 was on hand covering the activity for the day's news community spotlight feature. They had come out every year to help bring awareness to the case. The anchor reminded everyone that Josalyn was missing but not forgotten while encouraging donations. There were activity stations, bounce houses, food, face painting and more. Police officers walked through shaking hands and answering questions.

"Mrs. Mabrey."

"Yes, Gay where are you. We've been looking for you."

"I got caught up at the station."

"Is everything ok? I haven't seen detective Graham either."

"Everything is fine." Gay tried to hide the emotions in her voice.

"Can you and Tony meet me at the hospital?" Josalyn was being transported to the hospital to be examined. Gay sat in the back holding her hand the entire way.

"Hospital?"

"Yes, I had a minor fender bender but wanted to share some information with you because it looks like I'm not going to be leaving here anytime soon."

"So it can't wait. You know we have all these people here and the news. Can I send Tony?"

"I know Mrs. Mabrey but I really would like you both to be here when I give you the information."

"Ok we will be there as soon as possible."

***

The local news had caught wind of Josalyn's rescue, which they called nothing short of a miracle. They had made it to the hospital before the ambulance. There were only a handful of reporters and a few cameras but enough to cause a stir. Josalyn was given a private room due to the sensitivity of the case. The Florida Bureau of Investigation had arrived as well but waited on the Mabreys to grant permission to question her. Doctors and nurses moved in and out. A few nurses had left their post out of curiosity. They had known about the case. Many assuming she was dead or would never be found.

"Gay, we're here by the emergency entrance. They don't have you listed as a patient."

"Hold on. I'm headed that way now."

"What is going on? What's all the commotion about?" Mrs. Mabrey asked.

"You will see in just a moment." Gay smiled through the tears holding her hand she led the way down the hall to a room off the side of the ER.

Josalyn was lying in the bed with her head turned away from the door. The lights were dimmed. On the way over it had been discovered that she was kept in little or no light the majority of the time and had developed a light sensitivity.

"There is your baby." Gay opened the door and pointed.

Mrs. Mabrey didn't move. She couldn't move. Tony stepped around her and looked at Gay and then at the bed. Josalyn had now turned around and was facing them both. There was not a dry eye in the room. Mrs. Mabrey began to weep loudly. She continued to stand at the door.

"It's ok momma. It's ok." Gay put her arm around her and helped her to Josalyn's bedside where Tony was standing. He too didn't speak. He stood looking at Josalyn who was now crying again.

"Is that Josalyn?" Mrs. Mabrey asked in disbelief.

"Yes, that's your baby girl. We found her. She's alive."

"She's not dead?" Mrs. Mabrey asked overwhelmed to a point her questions were illogical and irrational. Josalyn was right in front of her in the flesh and her mind refused to grasp the reality of it all.

"She's right here. Alive." Gay moved her hand to touch Josalyn's face. "Feel. Do you feel the warmth of her face? Do you feel the wetness of the tears? She's alive."

"Josalyn?" Mrs. Mabrey asked again. This time Josalyn responded.

"Momma. This is your Jay Baby."

At that moment Mrs. Mabrey lost it. She let out a long wail then she screamed to the top of her lungs. "Thank you! Thank you Jesus."

Tony stood weeping silently. He finally reached over and hugged Josalyn lifting her half way off the bed. "My baby. My baby." Where the only words spoken.

The doctors, nurses, and investigators left the room. Gay stood in the corner watching. She thought she knew God was real but at that moment she really knew.

THE TAKEDOWN

The Hawks now had boots on the ground in LA, Las Vegas, and Tijuana. Months of laboring and fact-finding revealed that the traffic moved within this triangle. While divorce proceedings were going strong between Parker Monroe and his wife, he laid low, but made sure the funding was there to keep things moving. Through a series of phone taps and email infiltration the Hawks were able to deduce that Mr. Risner was in the process of delivering 10 kids to a buyer to be used for various things ranging from domestic work to sex work to overseeing girls that were already used as sex workers. They would keep them in Mexico for a few days before flying them out the country. It seemed to be a passport hold up. There was pressure to just turn it over to the FBI or even the Mexican police but corruption was deep and they didn't know who was on whose payroll. Time wasn't on their side.

"Jonathan. Don't forget I'm going to be headed to LA in a few days with the girls." Marissa stepped in the bathroom and leaned on the wall.

"How could I forget. You've been talking on the phone about it for the last month it seems like. Buying all kind of crap and running non-stop. I almost thought you were training for a marathon."

"It feels like I've been training for a marathon. If not that, something just as big, if not bigger."

"Something tells me you're not telling me everything about this visit. I mean you all go to LA all the time and never have I seen this much fuss."

"I can see how it would appear to someone from your vantage point. It's nothing to it. We all have new visions and goals for next year. Just want to get a mini vacay in before we go our separate ways. Well you know what I mean."

"Vision and goals huh?"

"Yeah, Olivia's getting married. Tressa's opening another office. Gay well you know… "

"Still trying to be faster than a speeding bullet, more powerful than a locomotive, and leap tall buildings in a single bound?" Jonathan laughed.

"Boy you crazy, but sure right. She's still on the Superwoman- badass tip. I think finding Josalyn Mabrey just blew her head up times 50."

"I ain't mad at it." Jonathan rinsed his razor and turned to Marissa. "Come here." He reached for her hand. "I'm just glad it turned out alright. Nobody got hurt. Nobody died and now we can all get back to being regular people. We have some pretty big goals ourselves."

"That we do." Marissa kissed him. She felt bad for lying but knew all the stops would be pulled on this last rescue attempt. She had to be out of her mind to go along because no one in his or her right one would.

Tijuana, Mexico was just an hour from San Diego. Most people, especially Americans, frequent Tijuana for the cheap goods. The area was known for its influence on the economy and culture in addition to the trade and manufacturing dominance as it relates to the Northern US. Influence. It's border has been touted as one of the most visited one on the globe. The influx and out flux of people made the perfect breeding ground for drugs and crime to flow in either direction. Well known as the birthplace of the Tijuana Cartel, the Hawks knew they were headed into dangerous territory. A lot of activity was taking place, with the Oaxaca Cartel reportedly most recently joining forces with the Tijuana Cartel. Only needing a passport, they had visited 4 times over the last six months forming alliances with a few rogue cops and a notorious street gang. They needed people who needed money, not only that, they needed people who knew the area like the back of their hands. These people also had access to weapons. The bill for this was racking up into the tens of thousands and was being paid by the business line of credit. Gay wasn't sure how she was going to pay it all off but that would have to be dealt with later.

***

"So is this the last supper?" Gay joked.

"Not funny." Marissa quipped. "But it may be for us for a while. You have taken over my life and I want it back."

"Yeah, yeah. You keep reminding me."

The Hawks along with Mike Rosebaum, John Leblanc and a few of their LA allies sat at the dinner table for an impromptu celebration of the return of Josalyn Mabrey as well as going over a few last minute details of what they had coined *Operation Take Down*. They had run this play and dissected every detail over and over since they learned that the transport would be taking place sooner than they thought. With Mike and John both being former

SEALs, Gay was confident that they would get in and get out without a hitch. They were trained to work in all kinds of environments and in the most extreme conditions. They would do most of the work and the Hawks would be responsible for getting the children to safety.

"Well Gay I think you have outdone yourself this time." Mike bragged. "When you first approached us what… three years ago about wanting to take your work in a different direction we were both like, ok. Let's see how long this is going to last."

"So you're admitting you didn't have any confidence in me?"

"Not saying that but you did come to us with these doll babies who looked like they would cry if they broke a fingernail."

Tressa smiled. "Don't let the smooth look fool you."

"You definitely fooled us. As the old saying go you can't bring a knife to a gunfight." Mike continued.

"Yeah and how does that relate to us?"

"Tressa, no offense but Gay was talking about at that time helping families find their kids. That kind of work requires a certain skill set and expertise, manpower, money and then some. We thought it was a cute idea for friends but really didn't see how you all were going to pull it off. I mean we're talking about dentist, salon owner… and."

"Engineer." Marissa interjected. "Yeah sound crazy right."

"Very." John agreed. "But you all have been doing it. Making all the right moves and for that at least one child has been reunited with their family."

"Well whoever won that bet owes me some money." Gay laughed.

"Seriously Gay, the work isn't easy and dealing with kids and families it can be taxing. Now we are here going after the big fish. So for that you should pat yourself on the back. Then go back to the little fish."

"And it's scary as hell." Tressa confided.

"We will be in and out before you know it." Mike tried to reassure her. "Let's look at this one more time." Mike pointed to the map and then go over our roles and positions. We're meeting with the others after this."

There were two maps. One detailing the location where the kids were being housed. The other was detailing the region and exit routes and any safe stops if needed. The house was located just outside of San Quintin approximately 10 miles from the main travel road. It sat adjacent to a vacant house. Surrounding by 10 feet tall brick wall on either side, the front of the house opened to the yard. From the front of the house to the road was approximately 50 feet. There were 2 guards on the front of the house, the back and guarding the road leading to the house. Mike had ascertained that the house received weekly food deliveries and that would be the way to getting in the house and getting the kids. On the route were designated safe stops where they had paid the owners to stop if needed.

"Ok- Tressa and Olivia. We will hand the kids off to you once we get them. Your only task is to get them from us and to the second van which should be pulled in front of the house by that time."

"They nodded." Having studied the map and the plans they didn't have any questions.

Mike continued to explain the movement and what was going to happen. He also gave a few worse case scenarios and contingencies. If anything, the worse that could happen was they would be arrested for trespassing and have their due process in the court of law.

"Due process in Mexicali?" Marissa had heard some horrific stories about Americans and the law over there.

"It will be fine. Let's not even think on that. Just stay the course." John suggested while waiting on Mike to back him up.

"John is right. We will take care of the heavy stuff and you all worry about the most important stuff... the kids. That's why we are here. Right?"

"You're right." Gay agreed. She too had been quiet listening. Taking it all end to ensure that she did not misstep. "I appreciate you guys."

"Thank us later. Go get rested and we will see you all just before dusk tomorrow."

***

The weather was nice. The temperature hovered around 75 degrees and the sun played hide and seek behind the mountains. The air was dry. Tijuana was noisy and busy. The hotel they were staying at wasn't far from the border. Looking out, lines of cars waited to be checked in or out. Inspectors walked the cars using vehicle inspection mirrors to search the undercarriage for any contraband that was attempted to be smuggled. Other people could be seen riding bikes along the roads, many of which were unpaved. Street vendors sold clothes, fruit, and other what nots.

The ladies talked through what would happen later that day and what would happen after.

"Have you spoken with Ms. Langston lately?" Gay asked trying to ease the tension with light conversation.

"Yes, last week. I called to check on her."

"How's she doing?"

"As well as to be expected I suppose. I think it really hasn't sunk in that her daughter was drugged and raped by young black men. One that she thought she knew well. People look at their neighbors and community members as family. Not danger."

"You're right. It's good that you're keeping in touch. I need to give her call."

"You should. She asked about all of you. She will forever be a part of the family. Just like Jackie and Tony."

"Yeah." Marissa nodded.

"Are we good for this evening?" Gay asked. "We are right here. If anybody wants to go home now I'm okay with that."

"This is the last hurrah. Might as well see it through." Tressa responded reluctantly.

"I'm in." Olivia followed Tressa. "I would like to pray before we leave and suggest everybody touch base back home."

"That right there makes me nervous." Tressa said.

"What?"

"They way you framed it. Like be prepared. This may be the last time you see or talk to someone. You didn't say those exact words but that's what I got from it."

"Sorry you feel that way."

Marissa walked to the window where Tressa was standing. "Big sis. It's gonna be ok. I don't want you to feel like you are being forced to do this and you don't have to go because I'm going."

"Duh, I know." The latter is exactly what kept Tressa there. She could not let her baby sister go into this by herself. "Olivia. You gonna lead the prayer?"

The ladies joined hands in the center of the room and bowed their heads. Olivia prayed. "Heavenly Father you would have not given us this task if you were not going to see it through." The reality of the entire situation was that it was Gay's baby, Gay's vision so if God had given it anyone it was her. "We pray a hedge of protection around us, the babies, Mike, John and all that are involved. We pray that no enemy, snare or weapon come before us. That all roads are well lit, that the ways are made accessible and open, that the guards are distracted and that we get in and get out successfully. That the children will be reunited with their families and loved ones. That we are reunited with our families as well. We ask that you get all the glory from this. In Jesus name we pray. Amen, amen and amen."

***

The van was twenty minutes late picking them up. The owner of the grocery story had mistakenly used the wrong one. The one they were set to use was being used for an in town delivery. Mike had not factored in a delay. There were no streetlights to light the way. The road was rugged and bumpy. It was so bad that John thought they would catch a flat before they got there. The second van was coming from the other direction with all the ladies together and a third would be at the first safe stop waiting on them. The second van was already in position to move when given the signal.

Sure enough, two guards stood watch on either side if the road leading to the house. The driver and passenger were both members of the street gang they hired to help. To avoid any flags on the play, they had to stick with people from the area. The van was outfitted with a freezer and a few extra compartments which Mike and John hid behind. "Slow. Don't make any sudden moves." Mike instructed from the side of the freezer before taking cover.

The guards stepped in front of the van both carrying assault rifles. The first guard waved a flash light and put his arm out for the van to stop.

"Slow and easy." Mike instructed again.

"Cuál es tu negocio?"

The guards didn't speak English but Mike understood them to ask. What's your business?

"Estamos aquí para entregar la comida a la semana." ¿Dónde está Ammado? No eres el conductor habitual y esto no es el mismo camión?"

The guards asked about the regular drive and the different truck.

"Ammado está enfermo y el camión está en el taller de reparaciones."

The driver went on to explain that Ammado the regular driver was sick and the other truck was getting repairs.

"Ok . Tenemos que inspeccionar y dónde está el proyecto de ley con el contenido ?"

When No One Came

The guards wanted a list of the food that was being delivered and to check the back.

"Claro . Aquí está la lista y Pedro se abrirá la parte posterior para usted."

The driver handed them the list while Pedro exited the truck to walk around the back. The second guard held the gun to him while he patted him down for weapons. The first guard asked the driver to step out and he checked in for weapons.

Mike and John stayed still understanding everything that was taking place. The back door to the truck opened and the guard stepped in with the flashlight. He called out for the other guard to come around and look as well. Holding the gun on the driver he did.

"Es sólo la comida . Un montón de comida . Radio a la casa que están surgiendo con la comida."

The second guard instructed the first guard to radio to the house that the delivery truck was on his way up. That was the all-clear signal. The first guard turned his back to walk towards the front when the driver tazed him with the modified watch. The passenger pushed the guard that was inside the back and closed the door. Mike and John leaped into action and disarmed him.

"Road Dog B. Proceed." Mike signaled for the second van to move in. That van carried more gang members who took the place of the original guards. Van B would stay behind until Van A made it to the house.

"Ladies are you ready?" Mike asked. "Now comes the really hard part. I need you all focused and ready."

"Do you have a visual?" Gay radioed to Mike.

"We see lights on top of the roof but are still making our way. Stand down and wait for me."

Shortly after Mike radioed to say there were more guards and a few extra non friendlies- two German shepherds. "What do you want us to do?"

"They are expecting a food truck. Keep going?"

"It's too dangerous this time." While the team had been in similar search and rescue operations, that one didn't feel right. Marissa pleaded again, "I think we should turn around. It's obvious we are dealing with some people who are smarter and faster than we are. There has to be some big money behind this operation. Nothing is laid out as before. Just look around. Five men on patrol instead of two, where did the dogs come from?"

"Let's take what we have and just turn it over to the feds." Olivia offered a viable alternative that was sure to ease any apprehension while in their minds ensured that the mission would be accomplished.

"It's too much red tape. We need them to move quickly. If not, this house will be abandoned or burned to the ground when and if they do make it." Tressa refused to back down. She had come this far. "And you all know damn well that's not going to happen without us being interrogated and them- the men in black starting their own investigation on us. Hell, for all we know, to them we are a bunch of overzealous wanna be vigilantes. This war on children is not ours to fight alone."

"Vigilantes?" Gay smirked.

"You know what I mean. Come on now let's get serious." Tressa sighed obviously frustrated. She was ready to make a move. Get in and get out.

"You sure you don't have balls? Because they get bigger every year." Gay continued with the snide remarks.

"It's called heart. I got it from you Mama bear. Are we done talking?"

Marissa rolled her eyes having previously tangled with Tressa. "We are across the border for God's sake... deep into cartel country and who knows what other illegal happenings."

Olivia continued to side with Marissa. "Right! We did just purchase some weapons. Lord knows I don't want to go to jail in Mexico. We're not trying to do some Set It Off kinda shit. We have all the evidence. We know it's s about four or five kids in there all under eighteen."

"There have to be more." Gay spoke as though she was deep in thought contemplating the next move while listening to the conversation around her.

"If there are more this very attempt to get them out could go one of two ways. We get them safely out or we don't then them along with God knows how many more kids would be trapped." Tressa painted the picture to be as dire as it was.

"Right, but who knows if the men in black aren't already on this?" asked Olivia.

"Believe me, if they were we would know about it."

The ladies were going back and forth so loud they missed the first time Mike radioed for them to come on. The driver hit the gas jolting them back to focus. "Your man is calling. They are in and it's time." There was no seat belt as the ladies bounced up and down in the cargo space of the van. "Hold on. It's about to get ugly." The driver howled and pressed the gas to the floor. His adrenaline pumping.

Gay wondered how 6 of them could take down 5 of them. Then she remembered John and Mike were on the job. Pulling in front of the house, an alarm was sounding but no dogs barking. Van A was pulled to the side with a member on their team on watch holding a gun in the ready position. The three men with them opened the side of the van. "Mike- John we are here. What's your location?" The alarm screamed and they knew their time was running out. Marissa and Gay, being the better shots, both grabbed a gun and took their positions. "Mike-John."

At that moment, Mike appeared on the front of the house with two kids. John came from the other side with three. "Come on!" He screamed to Tressa and Olivia.

Gay we're gonna do one more sweep because we don't see the other kids. Thought there were 10?"

"It's supposed to be."

"We're going in. You go around the right and Marissa left. Don't be afraid to shoot. We got 4 minutes and then we're out."

Tressa and Olivia ran towards the kids left standing on the porch. Their intelligence was off. All the kids looked to be 5 and under.

Tiny legs dangled at her waist while tiny arms offered a grip that only fear could know. With the smallest girl on her back and two girls on either side Tressa ran as fast as she could across the yard of the makeshift compound to the awaiting van. Fifty feet felt like a mile with the added weight. The girl on her right side hand was so tiny it slipped from Tressa's. "Keep going. I got her!" Olivia yelled running a few feet behind with her own precious cargo.

Scooping the girl in her arms, Olivia was a close second. The door of the van was still open and the driver was ready. Held high by the owner, the double barrel shot gun on the other side of the door was locked, loaded, and ready to kill in an instant. The driver revved up the engine. Olivia hoisted the last girl into the van looked at Tressa who was comforting the little ones inside and smiled. A shot rang out from the side and Olivia fell forward into the van. The children were screaming. A sixth unaccounted for man who was guarding the compound had fired a shot before he was killed.

"Go! go!" Marissa pushed Olivia into the van. "Drive damn it!" She could see Gay, Mike, and the others getting into the other van and assumed the headlights behind were them? Stopping at the entrance they picked up the two fake guards and headed in the opposite direction. They knew the folk that were headed that way were coming from the other direction from the police scanner.

"What's going on?" Gay radioed Van B.

"One of your ladies has been shot."

"Who? How? What happened to the bulletproof vest?"

"It was a clean shot through the side of the vest." The thick Spanish accent made it difficult to understand.

"Is she still alive."

"Barely."

"Tressa? Olivia? Who's shot damn it! Screaming through the radio Gay asked again.

"It's Olivia." Tressa spoke into the radio.

"No, no! That wasn't supposed to happen. Mike we need to pull over."

"Gay the entire fuckin' cavalry is on it's way. I've already called in to have the Mexicali police meet us at the hospital and I put in a call to the bureau to have somebody get here quick."

"We're losing her Gay. We're losing her." Tressa screamed. "You need to do something. She came here for your ass."

WHO WILL CRY FOR THE CHILDREN?

"State your full name and then spell it." Special Agent Thomas instructed. "Speak clearly."

"Gaynell Thibodeaux. G-a-y-n-e-l-l. T-h-i-b-o-d-e-a-u-x." The recorder hummed loudly as she spoke into it.

"State your age, address, and phone number."

"I'm 42 years old. I reside at 3332 Terra Shoates Drive. Carson City, Nevada. My phone number is 775... 326...0927."

"We are conducting a formal investigation into the death of Olivia Marston on October 27, 2003 in the city of San Quintin, Baja California. You are a key witness in this investigation. And it is pertinent that you provide thorough and complete detailed answers to all the questions asked of you. Do you understand?"

"Yes."

"This case isn't very new to us. We have actually been

tracking the players for some time. For at least 7 years now. What is quite interesting and remarkable to us was your ability, along with Ms. Marston, Marissa and Tressa Radcliffe to discover an operation of this scale in such a short time frame. The mystery is how you came upon the operation. Was it by chance or did someone key you in on what was happening?"

Gay didn't think it was remarkable or as many have said ballsy at all. "To be honest, we stumbled upon it. Through the course of investigating the infidelities of Parker Monroe, we followed him to LA for an alleged conference for real estate developers. During the course of our detailing, we documented a meeting with Mr. Frederick Risner and Rick Norman."

"Are you saying the men were becoming lax with their dealings?"

"I can't say that. This was the first time I observed them together. Marissa is actually the one who decided to dig deeper. Through her own private investigations she discovered that three men where involved in illegal gambling, prostitution, and human trafficking. She also, during the course of her investigation, was informed that you all along with the IRS were investigating Mr. Monroe for tax evasion."

"For you ladies to have uncovered the amount of intel that you did, we are still baffled as to how you managed to stay under and off our radar?"

"I'm not sure either." Gay responded as clueless as the Special Agent.

"Whose idea was it to cross into cartel country?"

"It was mine. I take full responsibility for that. I take full responsibility for the organization and execution of the rescue

When No One Came

attempt." Gay had nothing to lose at the point. Naja was now living full time with her father and stepmother in Maryland.

"Let's take a break." The last thing the agent wanted was for Gay to shut down. It had been 6 months since the incident and the investigation into all three men was ongoing. An indictment was soon to be handed down. Gay had been interviewed twice before and cooperated fully as she was now. The FBI wanted to ensure that her story remained consistent throughout.

The nearest FBI field office was in Reno. The Special Agent in charge had asked the ladies to come to the office within a certain time frame to answer questions. They did not call it an interrogation but elicitation. Gay was not being charged with a crime. She was careful to use cash for all transactions and her allies cleaned up on their end.

She rested her head on the back of the leather chair. Unlike the interrogation rooms at the police stations, the office was welcoming and reminiscent of a home office. The temperature was comfortable. All the furniture was made of cherry wood. A picture of the 43rd President George W. Bush hung on the wall behind the desk. The same picture hung in the main foyer. Rubbing her temples she sighed loudly. Every time she re-told the story, a little bit of her soul was chipped away. The blood on her hands was a heavy burden to carry although Olivia's family pointed no blame.

"Sorry to have kept you waiting."

"That's alright. I don't mind the quiet these days."

"I only have a few more questions and then you are free to leave."

"Ok."

"Did you have any assistance in Tijuana?"

"Yes, we found a few men that were vending on the streets who agreed to drive us around and scope the building out."

"You know that we know what you all did was more elaborate and well thought out. We recovered some maps, two-way radios and a few other things. So that leads us to believe that it was more than just someone vending on the streets."

"That may be true."

"It is true. We are on the same team here. I'm not the enemy."

"I get that. You do know that I know you have a solid case on Mr. Risner and Mr. Norwood. Now if the buck stopped there I can't really help you."

"You are right. But we want to help you find closure in this."

"I don't think I will ever have closure. The only justice we could ever think about getting has already been served, or soon will be. The man who killed Olivia is dead. The men who were the reasons we were even in Tijuana will have their day in court soon. We didn't leave empty handed. The mission was almost accomplished."

"Almost?"

"Yes, accomplished would have been everyone who went in coming out. That wasn't our reality."

"We will let you know when the indictment is handed down."

"Don't do me any favors. I'm sure the media will have that covered."

***

The air smelled musty and wet after three days of continuous rain. Red, orange, yellow, green, blue, indigo and violet arched across the sky. The rainbow was a beautiful end to the rain and an even more beautiful addition to spring. The seasons rolled into each other. Or maybe it was just the busyness of the last three years that made one feel like the years were passing them by. As soon as the new year came, a few blinks, and Christmas trees and lights were everywhere. Gay had vowed to stop and appreciate the journey on her way to the destination.

The patio was too wet to sit outside. Gay opted for a window booth. The Blue Lagoon was still the brunch spot of choice. "I will have a peach mimosa please." Gay placed her drink order, put her phone face down after a time check and looked out the window watching the cars pass by. Occasionally she smiled at the passersby. She had invited Tressa and Marissa to brunch a couple of times prior to today. Each time they declined. Another time check of her phone and the ladies were almost an hour late. Gay decided not to call. Beginning her second mimosa she looked out the window to see them walking in.

"Hello beautiful." She was already standing to greet them.

"Hello Gay." Tressa was short in her response but remained polite.

"Hello chica." Marissa was warmer. "You look good." They ladies had not seen or really spoken to each since the funeral. Gay tried reaching out several times to no avail. Tressa avoided her calls all together. Marissa answered but didn't have much to say. They ended holding the phone in silence before one of them made an excuse to end the call.

"You look good as well." Gay smiled. "Can I get some love?" Opening her arms for a hug Marissa stepped in and they embraced. This was a different kind of embrace. They hugged each other tightly just as a child would do after seeing his mom after a long day away at daycare.

The waiter walked to the table. Tressa signaled for him to come back. Gay and Marissa continue to hug each other neither wanting to be the first to let go. With her head buried in Gay's chest Marissa began to sob deeply. "I'm so sorry." Her voice muffled by Gay's chest. "I'm so sorry." She missed her friend. It was obvious.

Tressa stood up and placed her hand on Marissa's back and rubbed it. She too was now crying. It hurt her to see her baby sister hurt. Tressa knew that Marissa loved both Olivia and Gay. She resented Gay because of Olivia's death. She was angry with Olivia for going along instead of pulling out. She was angry that Olivia had gotten killed and left a fiancé behind. She was angry with Marissa for not being angry enough. She was hurt, angry, confused. She felt all the emotions of someone who was grieving the loss of a loved one.

"I'm sorry too." Gay cried. "I'm sorry too. I need you to forgive me Marissa?"

Looking around the semi crowded dining area, many faces had turned to watch them. Some of the patrons had begun to cry as well. The scene in front of them was raw and emotional. While they had not been privy to what was going on or what had occurred that led to the moment, they sensed it had to be something devastating for the ladies. That moment was extremely intense.

"I've already forgiven you. The question is can you forgive yourself?" Marissa stepped back and asked.

"I don't know."

"You're being honest and I guess I can't ask for more. But you owe it to yourself. This guilt that you're carrying can't be good on your mental and emotional well-being." Marissa attempted some reverse psychology.

"You're right. It's not good, but I will work my way through it."

"Promise?"

"I promise." Gay gave her word. "Tressa I know you are angry with me and you have every single right to be but can we meet in the middle?"

"Gay come on. No I don't have a right to be. The selfish and unreasonable side of me wants to make it all about you. Make it all your fault when I know good and well we all acted on our own free will. Now was that free will was swayed because of our friendship with you? I would say about 90% of it was. But that's neither here or there."

"Well can we meet in the middle to put our differences aside?"

"I don't have any differences Gay. Yeah, I think the way things went down was totally f'ed up. Do I think that things could have been done differently? Yes to all of that. But as I said before, that right I don't have. I'm open to calling a truce."

"I don't want you all to be bitter. I want you to be better."

Marissa took Gay's hand. "Only if you are willing to do the

same for yourself?

"I'm working on it."

"I'll take that." Marissa gave a slight grin and asked for Tressa's hand as well. She looked at both women and spoke from the heart. "It has been a hellacious past few months for all of us. What surprised me most was the revealing of crack in our foundation. The crack in our friendship. I never imagined in a million years that tragedy would strike our friendship, our family, the way that it did, but even beyond that I never imagined that we would let that tear us apart. The time when we should have been strongest, we were weak."

The women had cried enough tears to last a lifetime, yet they continued to fall. The road to healing would be long but the gathering was a start. The whole notion was farfetched but to think that the call that started it all validated the hours spent away from home, the missed days from work, the conflict with loved ones and sleepless nights were not in vain. The discovery of one of the largest trafficking rings validated it was not in vain. Olivia paid the ultimate sacrifice. Her tombstone said it all, John 15:13, Greater love has no one than this: to lay down one's life for one's friends.

"I'm sorry. So sorry." Gay squeezed their hands.

"We are too." Marissa spoke for both of them.

"I have something for you." Reaching into her purse Gay pulled out two silver boxes tied with metallic bows and handed one to each of the ladies.

"What's this?" Marissa asked.

"Open and see."

The ladies both held the boxes in their hands for a moment. Tressa being closest to the window looked out and Marissa looked at Gay. "Tressa you first." Marissa nudged.

"Why don't you open them at the same time?" Gay asked.

The boxes held a silver necklace with a single canary yellow diamond. "Is this what I think it is?" Marissa asked.

"What do you think it is?"

"Olivia's engagement ring was made of canary yellow diamonds."

"Yes. Mrs. Marston had offered the ring back to Cato. He suggested that she keep it and make something nice out of it that she could wear in remembrance of Gay. She called me and asked if I would make something nice out of it for the three of us." Ironically there were three diamonds of the exact same size. "I had the stones removed and mounted on a necklace for each of us." Gay reached in her shirt and pulled out her necklace. It was identical to theirs.

Tressa placed the necklace in the palm of her hand admiring its beauty. It was bitter sweet. She looked at Gay and smiled. Her thoughtfulness warmed her heart to the point it was full. "This is beautiful. Thank you for the thought, love, and time you put into making sure we had a part of Olivia. Yes, the memories will always be with us. But this is…" Tears flowed again.

"I know. I know." Gay touched Tressa's other hand.

"I knew that Cato was a good catch." Marissa smiled. "Thank you Gay. I agree with Tressa. This is everything."

"Welcome. Can we eat now?" Laughing the tears. "All this crying has wore me out!"

"Sure what are you having? The usual with extra everything."

"Greedy Gay! That sounds about right." Marissa joked. "And were you here before us?"

"You noticed? An entire hour and 15 minutes."

"Mark your calendar Rissa because this will not, I repeat, will not happen again."

The Blue Lagoon was still their spot. The place where it all began was now the place where it all ended and strangely a place of new beginnings.

"Too funny!" Gay laughed followed by a long exhale. The world was turned right side up. If only for that moment.

***

St. John's Missionary Baptist Church was transformed into a mock television set. There was an audience, a stage, and a panel with a big screen behind it. The slide show rolled with pictures of missing black boys and girls all under the age of 21. Some of the images were professional headshots, others were images where the family was cropped away, others were of poor quality and some read only image available. This alone spoke volumes to many as the backgrounds of the missing children. If a picture was worth a thousand words, the words used to describe them ranged from happy, sad, poor, loved, trouble, fast, and the list went on. The focus of the television special that would air on BET was missing black children.

The Hawks had been asked to be a part of the special after Josalyn was found, along with a representative from law enforcement and a local nonprofit that was doing the work on the ground to locate and bring children of African decent home safely.

Gay wore a blue and green dress with a green ribbon. The green ribbon had become a part of her daily attire whether she was dressed down or dressed up. It was a conversation starter. Looking out she saw her mom, Tressa, Marissa, Cato, Jonathan, Naja, Mike, John, Josalyn, Ms. Langston and so many others who loved her and supported her.

"Thank you all for joining us to discuss an issue that is important to our community but receives little to no attention." The moderator greeted the panelists. "Let's start with you Special Agent Bradshaw with the Florida Bureau of Investigations. "Please tell us, on average, how many people under the age of 21 are reported missing annually and out of those how many are African American or black?"

"First of all thank you for inviting me and secondly thank you all for highlighting the issue of our missing black children. I'm going to quote the statistics as they have been reported. According to the National Center for Missing and Exploited Children, roughly 800,000 children are reported missing each year in the US. That would be roughly 2,000 each day."

"That's staggering. Of which how many are black.

"Nearly 20 percent of those reported missing are African-American. That's about 160,000 Black children reported missing each year." Gasps could be heard coming from the audience. The number was alarming and one that any layperson would not be aware of.

"I don't think we hear about these cases on national level."

"You won't hear about these cases. The local news may provide coverage and then it's lost when the next big story hits."

Special Agent Bradshaw offered an honest opinion.

"Ms. Thibodeaux. Thank you for joining us. You have had quite the year. Tell us how you got started doing this work, looking for missing black children?"

"I'm humbled to be here. To be honest, I didn't choose this work. It chose me. A little over three years ago I received a call from a distraught mother. A desperate mother who had exhausted all her resources within the town she lived to find her missing daughter. At that time her daughter had been missing for well over a year. There were no leads, no support, no coverage."

"Are you trained to do this work? How did you know how to help?"

"I'm trained to find people."

"Ms. Thibodeaux, who was the mother who called you?"

"Mrs. Jacqueline Mabrey called me."

"Did you think that her daughter would ever be found?"

"To be honest I didn't know. I do know the first three hours are the most critical. I do know that according to the Center for Missing and Exploited Children that the murder of an abducted child is rare."

"We appreciate all the facts and statistics you are providing for our viewers. Mrs. Zelda Jones your organization, Operation Black Rescue works to connect the dots with the media and the families of missing black children. What do you feel is important for those in the media to know as well as families?"

"I would like to address families first. I think it's important for you to have an up to date picture of your child as well as physical information. It can be a school picture, a phone photo, something. The biggest complaint from media is not being provided the information. Some things we can control, others we can't, but this one we can. That eliminates one excuse for not getting coverage."

The largely African American audience verbalized their agreement with what was being said.

"Beyond that I feel that those in the media should be more compelled when a human life is involved, regardless of race and socio-economic status. It can't always be about the ratings; and when the stories are told, don't make them all bad. Nothing pains me more than to see a story about a missing African American male or female and the only pictures that are shown are of them in an unfavorable light or they are characterized as being anything other than someone's child. It's not only hurtful to the families and the communities but it's wrong."

"Yes!"

"Preach!"

"Say it Sister!"

The audience continued to show their approval for the panelist.

"I see you are very passionate about this. Yes, very passionate. US television networks as well as local networks and print media can not continue to devote so much air time to the disappearances of one race without the other. There have been times where the media was saturated with coverage of children. During those times the children didn't look like ours. The disproportionate coverage does nothing to bring our children closer to home."

"Thank you for that passionate plea for fair and unbiased reporting. It doesn't seem like much to ask but time will tell."

The moderator added her thoughts. "Thank you again for your bravery, your courage, your commitment. We will now take questions from the audience."

***

Gay stayed and answers questions until the last person left. A few people had heard about her rescue mission in Tijuana and wanted to know how she did it. Some of the stories that were repeated to her were quite bold. Stories of grenades, shootouts and other humanly impossible feats. She laughed at the thought of how news travels from person to person and how when it does get back to the owner, the story had changed a hundred times over. She didn't divulge the truth either way. The impending indictment prevented her speaking about the case. For that she was glad. It was painful part of her life she would rather leave in Baja California.

"Ready?" Gay did not hear or see Marissa approaching and it caught her off guard. She jumped slightly.

"So we are letting guards down now?"

"I thought we could do that in church? If you're not safe here where are you?"

"Point taken. Ready?"

"Looks like we are having an impromptu family reunion. Everyone's waiting on us back at the house. You know Jonathan has thrown all the way down."

"I bet."

"That's if you are up to it?"

"I think it would be nice. Can I have a few more minutes? You know I don't get to see the inside of this pace often."

"There's goes another thing for you to add to your list. It's healing. It's good and maybe one of the best places to be on earth, next to a beach sipping a ... well you know."

"Yeah heathen, I know." They laughed at each other. "See you in 5."

The stillness of the sanctuary was calming. There was no confusion, no hate, no judgment, no fear. Gay looked around at the rows of pews and imagined herself when she was child singing in the choir on Sundays searching the congregation for her momma's face. She was Dynasty Langston. She was Stephanie Davis. She was Malika Henderson. She was the countless black woman and girls who were missing and forgotten. Then she looked at the choir stand. She was Doris Langston, Jackie Mabrey, Felicia Sims, Melissa Alexander. She was Gaynell Thibodeaux the mother of a black daughter whose life mattered.

She wanted the world to weep for them. She wanted the world to weep for her. She was finding her peace in the valley.

"Gay Thibodeaux."

"Is this Gay Thibodeaux of GT Enterprises?" The caller asked again. Her voice was weak.

"I need you your help. My son has been missing for three months now."

ABOUT THE AUTHOR

Skyy Banks is an author, entrepreneur and activist. She is a staunch advocate for HIV/AIDS awareness for women and girls, and is driven to educate and empower others on positive life style behaviors as the stat of Georgia's Red Pump Project Ambassador. A prolific writer, Skyy has written for online and print publications as well as HIV/AIDS prevention organizations. Her previous novel is Soul on Fire. Skyy resides in Atlanta, Georgia with her family and her beloved puppy.

Skyy Banks

CPSIA information can be obtained
at www.ICGtesting.com
Printed in the USA
FSOW02n1835060515
6960FS